Mr. Right-Enough

This book is dedicated to Dave Barker, the inspiration for this book; to my dad who was always my biggest supporter, to Judi, my "Sophie," and last but not least to my Bill, my Mr. Right.

Mr. Right-Enough

Samantha Hoffman

To my Mr. Right.
With love,
Samantha

Cover designed by Miggs Burroughs

ISBN 978-0-557-47577-3

First Edition

This book is based on some true events but is a work of fiction. All persons appearing in this book are fictitious and any resemblance to real people, living or dead, is entirely coincidental. Well, not entirely coincidental but all of the characters are composites of people and the author's imagination. That's the great thing about fiction; you can make people who you want them to be and invent things to make the story more interesting.

Chestnut Street Publishing, Chicago, Illinois

One

When you're 20 or 30 or even 40 you can't imagine being 50. But all of a sudden there it is, smacking you in the face and you think, "Holy shit, how did that happen?" It's better, as they say, than the alternative but really...holy shit.

I thought maybe I could ignore my fiftieth birthday and it would go away but Michael, my significant other, called on his way home from work, bursting my balloon of denial.

"Let's go to that new sushi restaurant for dinner tonight," he said. "What do you think?"

"We don't have to go out tonight," I said, thinking that crawling into bed and pulling the covers over my head would be a better alternative. "We're celebrating at my folks' tomorrow."

"I know, but we should celebrate today. It's not every day you turn fifty."

"Thank god," I said, examining my face in the hall mirror, pulling back sagging skin on my neck with my free hand.

Michael and I had been together nearly two years. We didn't live together but traded off staying at each others' houses several times a week. It was a nice arrangement and we had a sweet, comfortable relationship, far more peaceful than any relationship I'd been in before, including my two marriages.

We'd planned that he'd stay at my house tonight but I was thinking we'd spend the evening quietly at home with a nice bottle of wine and take-out from my favorite Szechwan restaurant. But Michael sounded so pleased with his sushi idea that I agreed. It was just dinner out, after all, not, I knew, a surprise party. I'd made him swear more than once that he'd never do that to me and Michael was a man of his word.

Now, while I waited for him to return phone calls and take a shower, I turned on my computer, double-clicked the AOL icon and heard, "Welcome! You've got mail!" I loved that. It was like winning a little prize.

An email from my mother said,

> **Happy birthday, Libby. I can't believe you're 50! It makes me feel so old.**
> Tell me about it, I thought.
> **I'm making some of your favorite things for dinner tomorrow. Come over about 6. By the way, I saw this article on retirement planning and thought you might be interested.**

She'd attached a link to an Internet article titled *Retirement Planning for the Single Woman*. My dressmaking/tailoring business was thriving but since I'd quit my corporate job as a graphic designer six years ago I could never convince my parents I was financially secure. I think they worried that my clients would dry up and I'd end up living in a cardboard box under an expressway. Or worse yet, at their house.

I answered emails from clients, checked an eBay auction and then I scanned the AOL welcome box with news briefs and weather forecasts and "Best Cities to Retire In." At the top was a hyperlink for SearchForSchoolmates.com and I smiled at the picture of a girl who could have graduated in my high school class in the seventies. She wore a dark turtleneck sweater with a locket on a small gold chain, and had long straight hair parted down the middle, exactly like my own senior picture.

I navigated to the website, typed in the name of my high school, the years I attended and my own name, Elizabeth Carson, and a list of 104 alumni from my graduating class came up. Familiar names jumped out at me; Mary Blevins, Susan Caldwell, Danny Davis. I could picture Danny's blond hair and dazzling smile and wondered if he was still cute or if he'd gotten fat and wrinkled.

Page two was more of the same and vague memories swam through my brain. It had been thirty-two years since I'd seen any of these kids. The thought that these *kids* were all fifty now made me wince.

I was on page three when I saw a name that warmed my heart. *Patrick Harrison.* Patrick had been my first love, the one I'd thought I couldn't live without. He was the bad boy with long hair, the one my parents didn't like and I couldn't resist. I remembered how we'd walk through the tiled halls holding hands; how he'd drop me off at my classroom, kiss me goodbye, and my heart would just about beat out of my chest. I thought I'd never survive until the hour passed and I could see him again. I could clearly recall that sweet terror, the heart palpitations, the blush that started at my chest and infused my whole body when he walked toward me. Was it possible to feel that way at fifty, I wondered, or did that only happen to teenagers?

"Libby," Michael called, "you about ready?"

"Be right there," I said and saved the SearchForSchoolmates.com website to my *Favorite Places*.

Michael seized a piece of sushi with chopsticks and popped it into his mouth.

"Raw fish good," he said in his best caveman voice.

While we waited for our dessert of green tea ice cream Michael told me about new houses for sale and a demanding new client he'd just started working with. He was one of the top real estate agents in the city and while I admired his dedication he always gave me more details than I cared to know. So now I nodded and smiled and thought about Patrick Harrison, wondering what he did for a living. I couldn't imagine. Definitely not an attorney. Definitely not an accountant. I knew I was going to send him an email but what would I say? *Hi, remember me? Remember when we slept together on New Year's Eve when we were seventeen?*

The slender Japanese waitress brought two tulip-shaped glass dishes, each containing a perfect scoop of green tea ice cream. Mine had a sparkler twinkling in the middle.

"Happy birthday," she and Michael said in unison. I braced myself for them to break into song and blew out a relieved breath when they didn't. I pulled the sparkler out and we both dug in, remarking how yummy it was; cold and creamy. Then Michael put down his spoon, reached into his pocket and placed a small black velvet box in front of me. I blinked at it.

"Open it," he said pushing it closer.

I didn't want to. I had a bad feeling. It was surely a ring but what kind? Hopefully a cocktail ring. Or a friendship ring. A wisp of trepidation wrapped around my throat.

The waitress and two busboys stood watching from a respectful distance, grinning like kids with a new Game Boy. "Go on," Michael said.

What could I do? *Refuse?* So while everyone watched I gingerly lifted the little lid. There, like a searchlight, sat an enormous diamond ring. My mouth fell open. The waitress clapped her hands together.

"Will you marry me, Libby?"

I stared. *Marry* him? Fifty percent of all marriages fail, I thought. Not to mention one hundred percent of mine. What was he thinking? "My god, Michael, it's huge." What I wanted to say was, *What the fuck, Michael? If you wanted to get married couldn't we have talked about it privately instead of turning it into a spectacle?* "How could I wear this? It's bigger than my fist," I said. He laughed. "You shouldn't have bought this, Michael. I'm too old for an engagement ring." And I don't want to marry you, I thought. I don't want to marry you or anyone else. Marriage doesn't work for me.

"You're never too old for diamonds," he said

Well, of course I knew that, but still...

I noticed then that the only sound in the restaurant was the faint clanking of dishes from the kitchen and I looked around to find five or six tables of patrons watching me. A plump, gray-haired woman in a flower-print blouse smiled encouragingly. A small blonde girl sat on her knees, arms crossed on the back of the chair. It was like a movie set and Michael was enjoying being the center of attention as the romantic male lead. What was I supposed to do now? How could I say anything other than yes with all these people looking on?

"Put it on," he said. I hesitated. "Go on." I took it out of the box. I made a show of it being too heavy to lift. Michael and our little audience laughed. When I slid it on my finger his eyes sparkled and he leaned forward.

"Well?" he said. "Will you?"

I held up my hand and made another show of being blinded by the glitter. The crowd loved it but I was just stalling, trying to think what to do. The silence enveloped me as they all waited for my answer. I had a quick vision of taking off the ring, putting it safely in Michael's hand and then running like hell out of the restaurant, disappearing down the street, maybe going into witness protection. Instead I said, "How could I not want to marry a man who would buy a ring like this?" Not a yes, I reasoned. An answer I could explain away later when I told him what I really meant was no.

The waitress let out a little squeak and there was a spattering of applause.

"Did you pay these people?" I asked.

Michael's smile illuminated his face like a sunrise. He got up and came over, put his arms around me and pulled me close. "I love you, Libby," he said and kissed me.

As I kissed him back I waited for the tingle, the blush, the thrill I'd felt with Patrick Harrison so many years ago. It didn't come. What came was like a solid mass settling in my chest. Shit, I thought, what have I done?

"You've made me a very happy man," Michael said, his eyes crinkling with pleasure. "We'll have a great life together." He laughed. "Well, we already do, but somehow it feels different now. Don't you think?"

"Yes," I said. "It definitely feels different."

Two

I'd never seen Michael as animated as he was on the short ride home. It was a little unnerving. Michael was not typically an animated kind of guy; he was typically relaxed, steady. He wasn't emotional or showy, he was calm, quietly intelligent and reliable. But I could only describe what he was doing as chattering, and Michael was by no means a chatterer. He was fifty-nine years old, for god's sake. Definitely not a chatterer. But now he went on and on about how he'd researched jewelers before shopping for the ring, the other rings he'd considered, how he'd learned about the four Cs of diamond buying. "Cut, clarity, color, carat," he told me proudly.

I couldn't help asking, "So how many carats," even though I didn't want to encourage him.

"Three." He smiled. "I would have gone bigger," he said, "but the jeweler convinced me that since your hands are small a larger diamond would overwhelm them."

I was already overwhelmed.

He continued the chatter. I would have been amused if I didn't hate the whole situation so much. I sat silent, cowed by his enthusiasm, feeling backed into a corner. How could I tell him I didn't want to marry him, that I didn't want to get married at all? I'd already been married, twice, and it hadn't worked for me. Michael always said he understood that and was fine with it. What the hell happened here? Now, amazingly, he was under the impression I'd said I would marry him and he was excited, as excited as I'd ever seen him. How could I break it to him? It felt cruel to throw cold water on such unbridled and uncharacteristic enthusiasm.

At my house he pulled me into his arms and told me again how happy I'd made him.

"Michael…," I began, feeling the walls closing in.

"I know, I know," he said laughing. "I'm acting like a school kid, aren't I? But I can't help myself, Lib, I'm so happy."

Oh god. I couldn't do it. I couldn't bring myself to be the dasher of his dreams. I couldn't bear the thought of his disappointment. I'll tell him tomorrow, I thought, in the light of a new day, once his excitement has ebbed and he was back to his normal, rational, sensible self.

I woke the next morning remembering I'd gotten engaged, and lay still hoping for a feeling of euphoria. All I felt was a slight dread. I didn't open my eyes for fear I would see Michael's face, all eager and elated, wanting to talk about a wedding; who we'd invite, what we'd serve, how much an open bar would cost, and I didn't want to discuss all that. I pictured a room full of smiling friends and relatives and then I pictured my middle-aged self in a tea-length dress trying to remember to keep my stomach sucked in and picking up reading glasses from a chain around my neck to read my vows.

When I finally worked up the courage to look I was relieved to find the bed empty except for Rufus, my cat, who ambled over when he saw I was awake and plopped his considerable mass down next to me for his morning scratch. I lay for a moment lavishing attention on Rufus before getting up to see what Michael was up to. But he wasn't there. He'd left a note on the kitchen counter.

To my fiancée,

He'd drawn a smiley face here. A *smiley face.*

I went to play racquetball, then I have a couple of showings, then a meeting this afternoon at the office. I might be a little late - might have to meet you at your parents' house as close to six as I can. I'll call you later.

I love you.

I immediately did what I always do in times of crisis: called Sophie, who'd been my best friend since we were fourteen.

"I was just going to call you," she said. "Happy birthday. I'm so glad you're older than me. So how does it feel to be fifty?"

"You'll find out for yourself in three months and you're not going to like it."

She laughed. "Three *long* months."

"So, Michael proposed last night and gave me a three carat diamond."

"Holy shit," she said. "Well, that's great. I'm excited. Just don't make me wear a pink dress with puffy sleeves again."

She'd been my maid of honor twice, but only once in pink. Both times in puffy sleeves, though.

"I don't think I want to get married, Soph."

"You said no to *three carats*?"

"Not exactly." I told her about the evening, how I'd felt railroaded into saying yes.

"Well, give it some more thought before you do anything. Don't get hung up on the way he did it. He was just being romantic."

"Michael's not exactly a romantic guy."

"I've always thought he had it in him. Think about it a little, Lib. Maybe the third time's the charm."

"Or not. Maybe it's three strikes and you're out."

"You can't count the first two," she said. "You married Jason when you were twenty, too young to know what you were doing."

"You were twenty-one when you married Pete and you're still married," I pointed out.

"I was always more mature," she said. "Besides, we're not talking about me. So, scratch Jason. And then you married Wally on the rebound so he doesn't count either. Michael counts. He's not like either of them. He'll be a great husband."

"How so?"

"He's solid, responsible, nice looking, kind. Should I go on?" She didn't wait for my reply. "Generous, sweet, smart, everyone loves him..."

"Okay, so I'll manage his political campaign."

"He's a good guy and he'd do anything for you and you get along great. What more do you want?"

"Shining armor? A white horse?"

"Oh, hon, that's for kids. And that stuff doesn't last anyway."

"So now I don't get passion, I get peace instead, is that the idea? Security instead of excitement? Comfort instead of romance?"

"Something like that."

"Is that what happens when you're fifty?"

"It's what happens, period. It's what you end up with anyway, if you're lucky. It's nice, Lib."

"Nice? It sounds pretty boring to me."

"This doesn't sound like you. What's this all about? You're crazy about Michael."

"I am," I said. "I think Michael's great. We have a nice relationship. And it's nice the way it is. But for marriage? I don't know. I don't exactly have that can't-live-without-him kind of feeling."

"Think about it, is there anything you can't live without at this stage in your life? Or any one? We're not kids any more. Think about your future. Think about having someone to share your life and grow old with."

"I do think about that." I pictured me and Rufus sitting in a rocking chair in a dim room that smelled of peppermint and cat food. "I haven't said no," I told her. "You're right, I do need to give it more thought. I will. Just don't tell anyone yet, okay? Not even Pete."

"I won't," she said.

Yeah, right.

Three

    I laced up my running shoes after we hung up. It was a beautiful morning for a run and I headed out and down the hill toward the forest preserve path. The sky was a clear pale blue with feathered clouds off in the distance. I pulled freshness into my lungs and relished the peace.

    I ran past my favorite house, a white, two-story colonial with a wrap-around porch, a white picket fence, lace curtains in the windows, and window boxes that were filled with bright red geraniums in the summertime. I'd never seen signs of life but envisioned the woman of the house in a blue shirtwaist with an apron and pearls, serving piping hot pancakes with big fat squares of melting butter to her smiling, fresh-faced family. I'd always thought if a For Sale sign went up I'd buy that house and live happily ever after. I never thought about who I'd live happily ever after with, I just thought you couldn't help but be happy in a house like that.

    When I reached the forest preserve path it was quiet and I only passed a couple of other runners. Michael didn't like me to run this path. He thought it was dangerous for a woman alone and told me I should run on streets where there were people and cars. But it always felt safe to me, and peaceful, so I didn't tell him any more that I still did it.

The air smelled pure, like pine and sunshine, and felt cool on my skin. I thought about what Sophie had said and knew she was right, that I needed to give Michael's proposal serious thought before making a decision. It *would* be nice to grow old with someone. I *did* want that. But it was hard to envision living with Michael, for some reason, let alone being married to him, and what did that say about our relationship? In all the time we'd been together we'd only talked once or twice about getting married and those conversations had been casual and brief. We seemed to be on the same wavelength, liking our life together as well as our lives apart. It worked. It was good. It was uncomplicated.

My feet made a soft thump, thump, thumping sound on the dirt path. Leaves swayed in the light breeze. I thought about how I'd felt with Patrick Harrison so many years ago. There's a huge difference between being seventeen years old and being fifty, I knew, but I really wished I felt some of the passion, had just a smidgeon of that out-of-control feeling I'd had back then.

In all the excitement I'd forgotten to tell Sophie about seeing his name on the SearchForSchoolmates.com website. She'd get a kick out of it. His was one of those names we'd bring up in our nostalgic "Remember the time…" conversations.

The first time I'd seen Patrick was at a Christmas party my senior year in high school. I'd been talking to Sophie and her boyfriend Pete, now her husband, and I'd whispered, "Who's that?" when Patrick walked in. He wore black jeans and a black leather jacket with a silver chain hanging from his pocket. His hair was long, past his shoulders, much longer than the other guys, longer than mine. He looked dangerous to me, exciting, and very sexy. I could still remember that moment clearly in my mind.

Pete had waved him over and I'd stared at Sophie. "You *know* him?" She'd smiled.

"Patrick, this is Libby," Pete had said. Patrick's eyes were soft and brown, and bore into my soul when he smiled at me. When he took my hand a tingle ran up my arm. Our attraction was instantaneous and we spent the rest of the evening together, then New Year's Eve and then the rest of our senior year.

****

When I got home from my run I went immediately to my computer, did not even take off my sweaty clothes. I pulled up the SearchForSchoolmates.com website and clicked on Patrick's name. In order to send an email I found that I had to sign up and pay forty dollars, which I did without hesitation. Finally there was the email window with Patrick's name in the *To* box and mine in the *From*.

Patrick, I began. **I have no idea what made me go to the SearchForSchoolmates.com website but when I saw your name on the list it made me smile and I had to join just so I could email you. So you owe me $40!**
Do you remember me? How is it possible that it's been 32 years?
I have many fond memories of you. I remember your black leather jacket and your great smile. I remember dancing to Aerosmith and Badfinger. And I remember New Year's Eve at Jack Bradshaw's house when we were 17. Whenever

**anyone asks me about my most memorable New
Year's Eve that's the one I describe.
What's happened in your life? Last I heard
(20some years ago) you had moved to Florida. Are
you still there?
I hope you haven't forgotten me - I will be
crushed. I hope you are well.**

I signed it, wrote *Your past comes back to haunt you* in
the subject line and read it over again. Should I send it? If I did
would I tell Michael? Somehow I didn't think so. But what the
hell, I thought, and before I could change my mind I clicked
Send.

I laughed at the nervousness I felt. What was that all
about? Who cared? He was just a guy I knew a lifetime ago.
Big deal if I never heard from him.

But I hoped I would. I hoped he'd write back and say
he thought about me every New Year's Eve at midnight. I
hoped it was indelibly etched in his brain as it was in mine. It
was the night, after all, that I lost my virginity.

Four

I'd been so excited when Patrick asked me out for New Years Eve that year. We'd only been dating a few weeks and it was such a big deal date night. I'd never had a date for New Years before. We'd go to a house party, Patrick said, and I imagined us in a room full of other kids, dancing when midnight struck, seeing his face, the curve of his chin, just before he kissed me. I wondered what kind of kiss it would be; a long one in front of all those people or just a peck? A long, sweet one, I hoped. One that told everyone I was his.

"It's at Jack Bradshaw's house," Patrick said. I'd known Jack since third grade. Our fathers played softball together, our mothers bridge. He told me Sophie and Pete would be there but he didn't know who else, and I didn't care. All I cared about was being with Patrick.

Sophie and Pete were already at Jack Bradshaw's when Patrick and I arrived that night, and Jack's friend Frank, but no one else. Were we early? A table was laden with chips, sour cream and onion dip, cocktail weenies wrapped in pastry and Cheetos. A cooler with beer and ice stood on the floor in front of the table. It appeared that nothing had been touched except for the two beers Jack and Frank held. The Doors blasted from the stereo with *Light My Fire.*

"Where is everyone?" Pete asked as he shook hands with Jack and Frank.

"We're it," Jack said over the music. "Everyone else had something else going on. Said maybe they'd stop by later." Clearly this was not his first beer. "Frank and I are going out. You guys are welcome to stay. No one's home, folks are out - won't be back til the wee hours of the morning. Eat, drink, be merry. We'll be back later." And then they were gone. The four of us looked at each other blankly and then burst out laughing.

So there we were, just the four of us, seventeen years old, all alone in the empty house. Pete and Patrick each grabbed a frosty beer, clinked bottles and took a long swallow. Then they got one for me and Sophie.

"What the hell happened here?" Pete asked.

"How is it *everyone* had something else going on?" I said. "When did he ask them? *This afternoon?*"

"Well hey," Patrick said, "here we are in this big ol' house with food, beer, music and..." he looked at me, "... each other. Can't get much better than that."

"I'll drink to that," Pete said and we all clicked beer bottles.

There was a huge stack of LPs by the stereo and we looked through Jack's collection. He had all our favorites: Creedence Clearwater Revival, Bad Company, Steely Dan, The Moody Blues, Neil Young. We talked and laughed and listened to music. We danced to the rock stuff and a little later we put on some slow music and turned down the lights. It was cozy and warm in the basement rec room and having Patrick's arms around me made it even warmer. He held me close and kissed the top of my head. I loved the feel of his body so close to mine and the way he ran his hands up and down my back. I wrapped my arms around his neck and closed my eyes. It was a perfect New Year's Eve.

Sophie and Pete made out as they danced and I couldn't help watching them over Patrick's shoulder. I envied how easy they were with each other. Before long they disappeared entirely. After a while Patrick looked around the room and said into my ear, "Hmmmm, looks like we're all alone." It thrilled me and scared me at the same time. We sipped our beer and danced some more and then Patrick started kissing me, soft kisses on my neck and forehead. Then he kissed my lips and his tongue was in my mouth and there was no one to watch us and the house was quiet except for Elton John on the stereo. The lights were low and we sat on the couch, sinking into the puffy cushions.

His kisses were soft and his hands roamed my back and shoulders and into my hair, making my skin tingle. When his hand found my breast I couldn't concentrate on his kissing for the feel of that hand on my breast. But I didn't stop him. Part of me liked it but another part was ashamed that I would let him do this. We'd only known each other a short while. I wondered if that was what he'd been after all along but I'd had too much beer to think about it for long. Patrick moaned a little. Then he took my hand and said, "Come on," pulling me off the sofa and leading me upstairs, into one of the bedrooms.

"Should we be in here?" I asked, wanting to stall, wanting to run out the door and into the street and right home to the safety of my own bedroom in my father's house.

"Sure. It's okay," he said. He closed and locked the door and said, "All safe now. Is that better?" Not really, I thought, but I didn't want to be a prude.

Patrick pulled back the flowered, satin bedspread and sat down while I stood, not knowing what to do or say, and feeling conspicuous and awkward. I thought I should get the hell out of there before I did something I'd regret and I was eyeing the door for a quick getaway when he patted the bed beside him and said, "Come here," so softly and sweetly that I went right over and sat beside him.

"I'm not sure we should do this," I said in a small voice, afraid he would laugh at me. But he said, "It's okay, we won't do anything you don't want to do." I let him touch my breast over my sweater and after a little while I relaxed and kissed him back, touching his chest and shoulders and running my fingers through his soft, silky hair. And then his hand snaked up under my sweater and touched my breasts over my bra and then he pushed my bra aside and he was touching my flesh and my nipples and sending chills through my body. His breathing was faster now. So was mine.

As if I had done it countless times before I sat up, feeling bold, pulled my sweater over my head and removed my bra with a quick, expert movement. Suddenly there I was, practically naked. Oh Jesus. It was like I was possessed.

I heard a small moan in Patrick's throat as he looked at me. He got up on his knees and took his shirt off, and then he pushed me gently and lay down directly on top of me, our chests making acquaintance, his skin cool and soft. I loved his hands on my body and loved touching his strong muscled back and shoulders. I was crazed and breathless under him, and powerless to stop.

Patrick was slow and gentle, and a glow spread like melting chocolate from my very center to the tips of my fingers. When he pulled something out of his jeans pocket and the wrapper crinkled I knew it was a condom. I am really doing this, I thought. I am going to lose my virginity tonight.

Afterwards, as we lay side by side, my head in the crook of Patrick's shoulder, he asked. "Was it good for you?"

How would I know? My only reference point was *Peyton Place*. "Yeah, great," I said.

"You're beautiful, Libby."

I thought I would die of happiness. My heart wanted to lift right out of my body and float around the room. I wanted him to say it again. I wanted him to say he loved me.

Patrick got up out of bed and took my hand to pull me up with him. When I stood he held my hand out to the side and looked me up and down. I didn't flinch as he admired me. "Beautiful," he said. "Perfect."

I blushed.

"Dance with me," he said and took me in his arms. There was no music but my heart was singing so loudly I thought that's what Patrick was hearing. I was in heaven.

And then someone pounded on the door.

"Who's in there?" Jack Bradshaw shouted, his voice edged with panic. "Harrison, is that you?"

"Uh, yeah. Just a minute," Patrick called as we frantically grabbed our clothes off the floor, my heart pounding like a jack-hammer.

"C'mon man, outta there. Now! My parents are pulling into the garage!"

Thinking back on this now made me chuckle but it wasn't funny back then and my parents, of course, had found nothing amusing about it.

I'd been eating pancakes the next morning when Jack's mother called. My mom had picked up the phone in the kitchen and I froze when she said, "Margie, happy new year to you, too."

I watched her face and saw the moment Mrs. Bradshaw described last night. My mother turned to me and stared as she listened, her eyes saturated with disappointment. When she hung up she said, "Don't go anywhere," and left the kitchen.

This must be what it feels like to go to the guillotine, I'd thought, and cut my pancakes into tiny pieces, poured more syrup on top and mashed it all with my fork. By the time my parents came back and sat at the table, I was looking at a nearly solid, gluey mass. My mother eyed the plate.

"Mrs. Bradshaw says you and Patrick used their bedroom last night and left it a shambles," she said.

"It wasn't a *shambles*," I said.

"So you *did* use their bedroom?" my father said. I picked up the fork and mashed some more.

"Libby, I'm shocked at you. Is that the kind of girl you are?" my dad said.

Mash. Mash. Mash.

"You slept with that boy?"

Mash. Mash. Mash.

"You're too young to have sex," my mother said.

"We used a condom," I said.

"Well *that's* comforting," my father said. "I'm very disappointed in you, Libby."

"You don't understand," I said. "We love each other."

Where had that come from? The look on my mother's face reflected the surprise I'd felt after the words had escaped my mouth, but I hated that they were sitting there thinking about me in bed with Patrick, thinking I was a tramp.

I'd had to call the Bradshaws and apologize, and offer to buy them a new bedspread and sheets (which they kindly declined). I was grounded for a month.

"You will come right home after school and you will not go out on Saturday nights for a month except to work," my father had said. "Unfortunately I have no control over what you do at school but I don't ever want to see you with him again."

Of course we saw each other at school every day. For the month I was grounded Patrick picked me up at the bus stop in the morning and dropped me there after school. And after the month, when I could go out again in the evenings and weekends I spent all my time with him. My parents knew who I was with but they never asked and I never said. I'm sure they breathed an enormous sigh of relief the day I left for college. I'm sure they were most grateful that I hadn't gotten knocked up.

Five

Michael called later in the day to tell me he'd have to meet me at my parents' house that evening, that his meeting was running long.

"Should I bring anything?" he asked. This was the night we were celebrating my birthday with my family.

"No, I've got some wine. Do you have a second or are you in a hurry?" I asked, thinking to plant a seed about not getting married.

"I've got to run," he said. "George is waiting for me."

When we hung up I sat for a moment, thinking I should have told him not to say anything to my parents about our getting engaged. So I called back but got his voice mail. Well, I'd have to catch him when he walked in, I thought, and just tell him we should save the special announcement for another day. That we needed to talk first and work things out.

Later, when I went to get dressed to go to my parents', Rufus was asleep on my bed, looking like a big ball of gray flannel. He opened one eye when he heard me open the closet door. He yawned and stretched and then walked over to the edge of the bed where he stood meowing. My clothes hung neatly; jeans on one side, casual pants next, dress pants after that. Blouses then dressy tops then casual tops then skirts then a few dresses. In one corner were a few things Michael left at my house. A couple pairs of khakis, one pair of jeans and two shirts.

While I pulled out a pair of black jeans Rufus continued to meow. As I pulled them on he put out one paw toward me, waving me over. It was his game. He liked attention. "Pet me," he'd say if he could talk. "Just a little scratch around the ears." So I did.

I put on a sleeveless gold v-neck top, a wide leather belt and black boots, and pulled out a jacket with a black and tan pattern. Not bad for an old broad, I thought, looking at my reflection.

I was on my way to the bathroom to check my makeup and hair when I thought to look at my email and see if Patrick had responded. I didn't expect to hear from him so soon, it had only been a few hours, but a big smile spread over my face when I saw an email with an unfamiliar screen name, KayakDude, and the subject line, **Re: Your Past Comes Back to Haunt You.** I laughed out loud, feeling as if I'd just been invited to the prom, my heart thumping as I opened the email.

> **Libby**, it said. **Wow! You brightened my day. It's great to hear from you, and no, of course I haven't forgotten you. How could I? I've often wondered where you were and how you were doing. I looked for your name when I first joined searchforschoolmates.com and**

hoped some day I'd find it. And here you
are!

So, okay, here's my life in a nutshell: I was
married, then divorced and I have a son
who's almost 30. He's married and has two
little ones. It's amazing being a grandpa. Do
you have any kids? Are you a grandma?
Man, that's a concept.

You heard right – I did move to Florida and
I'm still here in a small town on the Gulf
coast. Like the rest of Florida it's growing
fast but we still have miles of undeveloped
sugar-white sand beaches. I have a sea kayak
tour business that I run in the summer plus I
own a couple of apartment buildings that
keep me pretty busy, always something to fix
or re-hab. Or a deadbeat tenant. But mostly
I enjoy it. I've had a great life.

Yeah, that New Year's Eve is one of my
favorite memories, too. Man, I'm flashing
back now and remembering when Jack
Bradshaw's folks came home early. Whew,
that was embarrassing, wasn't it? I'd
forgotten that part until now. Jack's mom
was pretty freaked out, wasn't she? I'm sort
of remembering that you got in big trouble
over it, too, but can't remember how.

Do you keep in touch with anyone from high
school? I haven't been to Chicago in years
and years. My parents moved to Florida not
long after I did and my brothers went out
west so I lost track of everyone. Do you ever
hear anything about Sophie? What about
Pete?

So glad you emailed me! I'm not so great at this typing thing (never took typing in high school – who knew guys would need something like that?) but I look forward to hearing from you again. Tell me all about your life.
Peace,
Patrick
P.S. Worth the forty bucks!

Peace. That sounded so much like him. The sea kayaking business sounded exactly right, too. No corporate crap for Patrick Harrison. I laughed delightedly. I had an image of him sitting at his computer, typing with two fingers, a cigarette hanging out of his mouth, long hair in a ponytail. It was silly really, how happy I was that he remembered me; like a kid with a new best friend. I could see his face clearly in my mind, his dark eyes and sweet smile. What did he look like now? Did he still have long hair? Did he have hair at all? Was he still cute?

I couldn't wait to tell Sophie. She would freak out. I wanted to answer the email right that second but only had time to read it over once more before I had to finish getting dressed.

As I checked my eye shadow, added a little more blush and brushed my hair I tried to see myself with Patrick's eyes. What would he see? A reasonably attractive, fifty year old woman with gray streaks in her curly brown, shoulder-length hair. Too much gray? Did it make me look old? Would he recognize me after thirty years? I thought I looked pretty good but what did I really know? How can you be objective about the face you've been looking at every day for fifty years?

* * *

Michael's car was already in the driveway when I pulled up to my parents' house, which totally pissed me off. Why hadn't he called to pick me up if he was going to make it on time? How long had he been there and what was he talking about. He'd better not have said anything about our engagement. If he had I knew I would lose it. I could image hitting him over the head with my purse. Not that I'm a hitter. I didn't really think he'd say anything without me but Michael was unpredictable these days and I was irritated by the possibility. My sister's car was there as well and I prayed the whole damned family wouldn't be exclaiming over the big news when I walked in.

The living room was empty. It was tidy as usual, with bowls of pistachios on the mahogany end tables.

"Where is everybody," I yelled.

"In here," my mother called from the back of the house where the kitchen, dining room and family room were. As I walked down the short hallway I heard whispering sounds and someone saying, "Shhhh." Goddamn it, I thought, he's told them. I was furious when I turned the corner, thinking what the hell I'd say, ready to deny everything, but was assaulted by shouts of, "Surprise!" as twenty or thirty people stood among black balloons (it wasn't until later I'd notice they were emblazoned with 50 or Over the Hill) and black streamers strung across the kitchen.

A fucking surprise party. Michael had sworn he'd never do this and yet there was his face, right in front with a big, proud smile. I wanted to slap him.

Six

I was overwhelmed with the amazing assemblage of people; family, friends, even a couple clients. How long had Michael been planning this? When did he begin thinking it was a good idea? Before or after he promised never to do it?

They were lined up as if at a funeral to pay their respects, hugging me, patting me on the back, wishing me happy fiftieth birthday, the birthday I'd hoped would pass quickly and quietly.

"So you were surprised?" my mom asked, which was, of course, putting it mildly. I'm sure she'd seen the shock (maybe revulsion) on my face, but wanted reassurance in that way people do when they're excited about a special gift and want to make sure the recipient shares their enthusiasm.

"Completely," I said.

"Oh, *good.*"

My dad wrapped me in a big bear hug. "Happy birthday, pumpkin. Hard to believe you're fifty. Seems like just yesterday I was teaching you to use a power saw." Strands of white hair made a valiant effort to cover his bald spot. His blue eyes sparkled.

I laughed. "Daddy's little tomboy." He and I shared a love of building things and fixing things and figuring things out.

"You don't look a day over twenty," he said.

"You're prejudiced," I said.

"You're right. Truth is you don't look a day over thirty." I laughed and kissed his soft cheek. My father was eighty-two but looked no more than seventy. He was tall and thin and had an energetic glow about him. He walked every morning and played golf whenever he could, spurning the use of carts.

"Happy birthday," my sister Jill said when she made it through the crowd. "I didn't like it when you went off to kindergarten without me or when you got to wear panty hose first or go to a movie with a boy, but now for the first time in my life I'm glad you're the oldest." Jill's husband Mark was with her, and their eighteen-year-old son Jason. She and Mark had been high school sweethearts, were married now for twenty-eight years and had three beautiful, well-adjusted children who considered Jill and Mark friends as well as parents. Two of their kids were married and lived out of town, and there were four grandchildren who, of course, were smart and adorable. Jill was the anti-Libby. I was the twice-divorced one, the unconventional one. She was the solid, responsible, dependable one. If I didn't love her and her family so much I could have hated them for all that perfection.

Then Sophie was hugging me, whispering, "Sorry. I told him not to do it, I swear." Pete handed me a large vodka on the rocks with two olives and said, "Drink up and you'll be fine."

My mother hadn't made any of my favorite foods as her email had promised. She'd ordered them: baby back ribs, jalapeno corn bread, potato salad, corn on the cob. I'm sure it was good food, everyone seemed to enjoy it, but I didn't have much of an appetite. Drank a lot of vodka, though.

Beatrice Rosatti, my favorite client, brought me a plate when I flopped down on the couch, the first time I'd sat all evening. Bea was a retired kindergarten teacher. She'd been married for forty-nine years until her husband had died in his sleep as he lay next to her five years before. She'd hinted that he'd died while they were having sex but I didn't pursue it, although I'm sure she wouldn't have hesitated to tell me. Now she had a boyfriend, Dominick, whom she'd met online.

Tonight she was splendid in a purple pantsuit (which I had altered for her), turquoise shoes and a chunky purple and turquoise necklace with matching dangly earrings. Her platinum blonde hair was pulled up in a complicated froth about her head with rhinestone clips strategically placed.

"You look like you need nourishment," she said unfolding a napkin on my lap. "Happy birthday, darlin'. Are you enjoying your party?"

"Sure," I said, picking at a rib. She raised a finely penciled eyebrow. Something in my tone, I suppose.

"Were you surprised?"

"That's an understatement," I said. "I told Michael about a billion times that I hate surprise parties and never wanted him to throw one for me." There's truth in too much vodka.

"Oh, my," Bea said. Dominick came over and handed her a glass of wine. He leaned over and kissed my cheek. "Happy birthday, dear girl. Having a good time?"

Bea and I looked at each other. She raised that eyebrow again and we burst out laughing. Dominick looked puzzled. "I'll never understand women," he said. "And I'm too old to start now." He was eighty-seven to Bea's eighty.

"Seems we'll have a lot to talk about this week," Bea said. "You're coming over, right? I have a lot of work for you."

"Right," I said. "We'll talk."

* * *

My mother had made carrot cake with cream cheese frosting. My favorite. It blazed with fifty candles.

"Somebody get a fire extinguisher," I said.

Everyone sang *Happy Birthday*, a few actually on key, and I blew out the candles before the house could catch fire. Michael started pouring champagne.

We hadn't spoken much during the evening, there'd been too many people, too much tumult, and Michael had been busy playing host, the guy who'd pulled off the impossible. I wasn't sure I liked this new, stealth Michael.

Once everyone had a glass he whistled loudly to get their attention, a piercing sound that caused people to wince. "A toast to the birthday girl," he said when it was quiet, holding up his glass. "To the best-looking fifty year old I know." Shouts of *here, here!* I think I blushed. Or maybe it was just a hot flash. "To the love of my life," Michael continued, clinking his glass to mine and we all took a sip.

But Michael wasn't finished. He whistled again, that same shrill sound. Everyone watched expectantly while my heart sank to my stomach, and before I had time to figure out how to head this off he raised his glass again and said, "To my future wife." Confused silence. Michael laughed and then practically shouted, "I proposed last night and Libby said yes!"

The place went up for grabs and I thought I was going to throw up. My Aunt Shirley let out a squeal, Uncle Charlie came over and thumped Michael on the back. Faces loomed before me like balloons, many with expressions of surprise, others with wide grins, the tinkling sound of glasses touching in the air. Another wave of hugs and kisses and now, "Congratulations," and, "It's about time." I could hardly breathe. Sophie watched me carefully, hoping, I suppose, that I wouldn't do or say something I'd regret later. Her daughters Tiffany and Danielle gathered around me, jumping up and down, begging to be bridesmaids, suggesting colors for the dresses. Ironically I was in the process of making the bridesmaid dresses for Danielle's wedding in a few months. As it should be – she was twenty-two and starry-eyed in love. The dresses, however, were an unfortunate shiny purple with big puffy sleeves and bows at the sweetheart necklines. And still I stood there thinking we could simply use those same dresses. That's what I was thinking. As if I would even have a wedding with bridesmaids; as if, even if I did, I would make anyone wear a dress like that. Clearly my mind had gone missing and I was operating in a haze of stupidity. And vodka.

If I could whistle like Michael, I thought, I'd do it and then I'd tell them all it was a cruel joke, that

Michael and I were not getting married. But I couldn't whistle. I could barely speak. What a mess. My whole family, all my friends, Michael's parents, my favorite client, all knew I was engaged. And they were all so damned happy.

Seven

It was another hour before people finally started leaving. Somehow I managed to get through it. And then, of course, I had to listen to it all over again when they said goodbye: "So happy for you," "Can't wait for the big bash," "Mrs. Dean. It has a nice ring."

I don't think anyone noticed the insincerity of my smile as I planned ways to murder Michael in his sleep. With each thank you I uttered my irritation grew like bread dough. I'd punch it down every once in a while and then someone would offer congratulations again and it would rise up even bigger.

"We need to have lunch," Jill said as she walked out the door. "I'll call you."

"Call me tomorrow," Sophie said as she and Pete left.

And then they were all gone, the house empty of everyone except me, Michael, his parents and mine; one big, happy family.

"I'm thrilled about your news," my mother said. "Welcome to the family, Michael." She kissed him and he smiled broadly.

"What kind of wedding are you going to have?" Michael's mother asked.

"We haven't gotten that far," I said.

"I'm very happy for you, honey," my father said. He put his arm around me and pulled me close. "Now I can stop worrying about you."

"Why would you worry about me?"

"You're my daughter. It's in my job description."

"I'm your *middle-aged* daughter."

"You're still my little girl."

"And my new daughter," Michael's father said.

Michael beamed.

"Okay, well, time to go," I said. Let's end on a high note, I thought.

We walked outside and Michael helped his parents into his car. I wanted to tell him to go home after he dropped them off, to his own house, but I knew he'd be staying at mine tonight. His *fiancée's* house.

He kissed me and said, "See you at home," and it was all I could do not to say, "*My* home."

* * *

I was pouring a couple glasses of wine when Michael walked in. He came in the kitchen and put his arms around me from behind. "My parents are so happy." I gave him a glass. "We should have champagne," he said. He was thinking celebration, I was thinking fortification.

"Let's go sit in the living room," I said. Michael brought the bottle. I sat in the wing-back chair near the fireplace and Rufus jumped into my lap and curled up into a fat, furry ball. Michael sat on the couch and patted the seat beside him. "Come sit here," he said.

"We need to talk."

"I know, but can't we do it side by side? Come sit with me." He was still happy. Completely oblivious to the fact that I was about to stick a pin in his bubble of joy.

"Things are moving a little fast for me, Michael." He paused, wine glass in midair, eyes searching mine. Rufus looked up at me and then at Michael. I scratched his neck. Michael drained his wine, then poured himself more.

"Fast?" he said. "You think three years is fast?"

"I guess it's how you did it, that you sprang it on me in the restaurant in front of all those people in spite of the fact that you knew I didn't want to get married again."

"I took a chance that after three years you might have changed your mind. And apparently you had. You said yes, Libby."

"I know, I'm sorry, Michael but I felt pressured." He sucked on the inside of his cheek. "And then you make a big announcement in front of our family and friends before I'm even used to the idea." I was getting riled up now. On a roll. "And you throw me a *surprise party* even though you promised me, *swore* to me you never would." Rufus jumped off my lap. I hated the words coming out of my mouth. When said aloud it seemed ridiculous, just plain ungrateful. Most women would love the kind of surprises Michael had planned for me.

"I love you. I wanted to do something special for you. Is that so terrible?"

"It's not that it's terrible. It's that you didn't think about how all this might affect me."

"I did, Libby. I thought about it a lot. I thought it would make you happy. I thought when you said yes you wanted to marry me, you meant it. So I figured you'd be excited to tell everyone and, okay, maybe I got carried away with my happiness and so I just did it." He leaned forward. "I'm sorry that I didn't clear it with you first. I'm sorry if that's not how you wanted to do it. I really am." I felt deflated. Stupid. Petty. "And I'm sorry you hated the surprise party."

"I didn't *hate* the surprise party."

"Everyone always says they don't want a surprise party but nobody means it. I really didn't think you meant it. I thought you'd have a great time with all your friends and family around."

I was suddenly exhausted. Every time Michael opened his mouth I felt worse and worse. His intentions were so good and all I could do was complain about it all. My indignation was in a puddle at my feet and in its place was a big pool of guilt.

"I love you Libby and I'm so happy we're engaged." *All right*, I wanted to scream. *Enough!*

"I love you too, Michael. I think I'm overtired. Too much excitement for the last couple days." He smiled. "Let's just go to bed and sort this all out tomorrow, okay?"

"You're not mad?"

"I'm not mad." Was I? Should I be? It didn't matter, I had no energy left for anger. We both got up and carried the wine and glasses into the kitchen.

"Let's have one more toast before we go to bed," Michael said pouring a splash into each glass.

Was he serious? "Michael, really, I'm exhausted."

"Just a little toast to our life together."

It felt like bees were buzzing around in my head. "Have you heard a word I've said?" Michael flinched. "I've had enough wine," I said. He looked at the bottle on the counter. "I'm overwhelmed, Michael. I've had enough toasts to last a lifetime and I am going to bed now." And I left him there in the kitchen with a wine glass in his hand and an expression of pure confusion on his face and I thought, *What is he, stupid?*

Eight

Michael got out of bed very early in the morning and I pretended to be asleep. He dressed quietly, kissed me gently on the cheek (I didn't move) and left to play raquetball. When I heard the front door close behind him I sighed. I wouldn't see him again until Tuesday or Wednesday since we rarely spent Sunday nights together.

Rufus came to take Michael's place, curling up against my side, draping a paw on my hip. I hadn't slept well but as soon as Rufus and I were alone I fell into a coma-like slumber. Later, after I made French Roast coffee and buttered a toasted English muffin I took my breakfast to my desk and turned on my computer. I reread Patrick's email and felt happy all over again. I was excited to answer it but first I wrote an email to Sophie:

What are Michael and I doing getting engaged? What are we, twelve? He's almost sixty years old for chrissakes. Next thing you

know I'll be having bridal showers and registering for china.
And that surprise party and the big announcement...kill me now.

The phone rang within ten minutes, as I knew it would. Sophie had a Blackberry so even if she wasn't home she was always connected. I gave her a hard time about how excessive and annoying that was, especially when we were having lunch or shopping and she was checking her Blackberry every other minute, but I loved it when I needed her.

"The party was fun," she said. "Even you looked like you were having a good time."

"Once I got over my initial irritation it was tolerable," I said. "But I don't understand why he did it knowing how I feel about surprise parties."

"I really did try to talk him out of it."

"I'm sure you did. Thing is, I was feeling okay about it, making an effort to enjoy it, even though I see no reason to celebrate turning fifty, and then he whistles for everyone to shut up and makes a birthday toast and that was fine and then he whistles again and I knew what he was going to do and there was no way to stop him then and I just felt sick."

"I know. But he didn't know how you were feeling, did he?"

"No. I didn't have a chance to talk to him."

"Well, so it's done and everyone knows. Maybe you should stop concentrating on what he did and really consider what you want. Think about how nice your life's been the last few years with Michael."

"I know. I have thought about that."

"It's been peaceful. It's been companionable. You enjoy the same things, you travel, you like each others' families. Michael's a man you can grow old with."

"God, you're like president of his fan club."

"Well, he's good for you, Libby. I just don't want you to do anything you'll regret. Just take a deep breath," she said. "Slow down. Give yourself some time to get used to the idea."

"Hey," I said, tired of thinking about Michael. "Remember Patrick Harrison?"

Of course she did. I told her how we'd hooked up and about our emails. "God, Patrick Harrison. That was a hundred years ago."

"I know."

"Libby," Sophie said, "is that what this is all about, with Michael?"

"No, of course not," I said. "It has nothing to do with Michael."

"Are you sure?"

"I am, Sophie. Do you think I would chuck everything because I exchanged emails with my high school boyfriend? First of all he lives in Florida, secondly I haven't seen him in thirty-some years. Plus, he wasn't my type back then, what would make him my type now?"

"What do you mean he wasn't your type? You were crazy about him."

"I know but it didn't last, did it? He was a hood. I was preppy. He majored in vocational ed. I was in college prep."

"Opposites attract."

"Only until I went off to college," I reminded her. "And then there's the minor detail that I have a life with

Michael and even if I don't want to marry him I like our life together."

"So, tell me about your emails," Sophie said.

She was pleased that Patrick had asked about her and Pete. Laughed that he was a grandfather. Loved his sea kayaking business.

"I wonder what he looks like," she said. "He was really cute thirty years ago."

"Probably fat and bald." I said.

"Tell him I said hi."

Patrick, I wrote after we'd hung up. **It was so great to hear from you. Isn't this amazing? Who would think we'd be in touch again after all these years?**
You, a grandfather – how is that possible? How did we get to be so old? No, I'm not a grandmother, never had children. I've been married twice (divorced now) but children weren't part of the picture(s). I wish they had been but life doesn't always turn out the way you expect, does it?
The sea kayaking business seems so much like something you'd do. I knew you wouldn't be an accountant or lawyer or some other "establishment" dude. Kayak Dude – perfect.
Yes, Jack Bradshaw's parents came home when we were in their bedroom – a very humiliating experience. Especially since they were good friends with my parents whom, of course, they called first thing the next morning. What a scene at my house that day! I think I was grounded for a year after that.

But, as I recall, we still managed to see each other.

Sophie and Pete got married and still are. They have two gorgeous daughters, one who's getting married soon. I'm a dress designer and seamstress and am making the bridesmaid dresses for the wedding. Tiffany, their youngest (15) is coming in for a fitting today. She looks just like Sophie did at that age, except she's got lots of piercings and a tattoo on her ankle. Sophie with an edge. They're a fabulous family. In fact I just got off the phone with Sophie and she says hi!

Do you ever get back to Chicago? Do you still have family here?

As for my life, it's been wonderful. Okay, yeah, I've been married and divorced twice but I consider that character-building. Now I have a significant other and we've been together almost three years. The other night he asked me to marry him and I have to say it shocked the hell out of me. I never thought I'd get married again but how could I say no to a three carat diamond?

Libby

Nine

Tiffany pivoted slowly as I pinned the hem of the purple confection she was to wear for her sister's wedding.

"I'm going to walk down the aisle in front of two hundred people looking like an iris on steroids," she said, surveying her image in the mirror, scrunching up her nose. "This is totally gross."

"You're going to look beautiful no matter what you're wearing," I told her. "Think of it as wardrobe. Imagine you're an actress and you're making a ton of money to make a movie about a wedding and just walk down that aisle like a queen. Like you're Julia Roberts."

"How about Britney Spears?" she said. "Just do a big cutout here in the middle so my belly button shows, rip off these stupid sleeves and lower the neckline. What do you think?"

Tiffany's hair, which used to be blonde, was a shade of red found most often on traffic signals, and clashed madly with the purple dress. She had a piercing through her eyebrow where she wore a small silver ring, four piercings in her left ear and two in her right. She had a tongue piercing as well, which glinted silver and made me wince when she talked. It amazed me that Sophie was so nonchalant about all this body-maiming. "All those holes will close," she'd say. "At least she's not into tattoos."

"So when are you guys getting married?" Tiffany asked.

"I don't know."

"Are you going to have a big wedding?"

'No, I'm too old for that," I said. "Besides, I've been married twice already. How many weddings does one person need?"

She giggled. "I think you should have a big wedding. I want to be a bridesmaid."

"I'd make you wear a dress just like this," I said, fluffing her big purple sleeve, "only in lime green. What do you think about that?"

She pointed her finger into her mouth and made a gagging sound.

"Turn," I told her and finished pinning the hem.

"I'm going to the movies later with Ryan," she said.

"Aren't you a little young to date?" I said, sounding like an old lady. It seemed like last week I was taking her and Danielle to Kiddie Land.

"I'm *fifteen*."

"Who's Ryan?"

"Christopher's brother." Christopher was the groom. "I'll be walking down the aisle with him."

"Well, fun," I said, hoping they'd still like each other by the time the wedding got here and realizing how cynical that was.

"He's hot," she said and blushed. Her smile was shy and her eyes sparkled. Young love, I thought enviously. I remembered those days.

"So how do you know when you're in love?" she asked. As if I knew.

"Oh honey, you're not in love. You just met him."

"So," she said. "Haven't you heard of love at first sight?"

"Sure, in books. In real life it's called lust." What was wrong with me? Was I really saying this to a fifteen year old? "Sorry sweetie. I didn't mean that. It happens. Just not often. And when it does you just know it," I said. "But being in love at fifteen is different from being in love at fifty."

"Were you in love at fifteen?"

"No. The first time I fell in love I was seventeen. And I thought it would last forever."

"What happened?"

"I went away to college and we lost touch," I said.

"Just like that?"

"Pretty much."

"How sad."

"Oh, well, things happen," I said. "But you should ask your parents. They fell in love when they were in high school. And look at them now. It can happen. But I think it's rare."

"How did you know you were in love with Michael?"

"I don't know," I said. "It's hard to explain. I just did." Cop-out answer, I knew, but thought it best to keep my cynical mouth shut. And how could I explain it to a fifteen year old when I couldn't explain it to myself?

When Tiffany left, I finished hemming her dress and picked up another. I wanted to finish the four dresses and deliver them. I was sick of looking at all that purple. It created a dissonance that was alarming in my normally cozy workroom, clashing with the pale yellow walls and burgundy carpet.

Later I checked my email and was warmed to see one from Patrick.

Libby,
You've been married twice and getting ready to do it again? Wow, either you're a glutton for punishment or an eternal optimist. Seriously, tho, congratulations. Yeah, I guess three carats can be pretty persuasive.
I came close a second time but got cold feet before we made it to the altar. I guess it wasn't so much getting married that scared me as that she was great but not someone I thought I'd want to spend my life with.
Do you have a picture? I'm attaching one of me with my son's family taken last summer when I visited them. Now, before you open it remember that I am 32 years older and almost that many pounds bigger than I was last time you saw me. So be kind. The heart's the same but the body sure isn't.
Hey, can I call you sometime? It'd sure be easier than typing, wouldn't it? And it'd be great to hear your voice. Here's my number if you want to call me. 850 555-6768.
Patrick

Call? Like on the phone? Stupidly, that hadn't occurred to me. It was as if he only existed in the virtual world. Now, realizing I could actually talk to him, I was unnerved. It was one thing to write, you could think about what to say before saying it. But talking? That depended on a mutual chemistry, didn't it? A connection. What if we had nothing to say to each other? I liked this little fantasy we had going. Why ruin it?

But hey, let's see what he looks like, I thought and quickly downloaded the photo. And there he was. I studied the current-day Patrick for several minutes, squinting my eyes to uncover the face I knew. It took some getting used to but he was there, familiar and not, all at the same time. I laughed out loud. Patrick had aged well. *He was cute!* Yes, he was heavier, his face was fuller than I remembered but he wasn't fat. And he wasn't bald. His hair was salt and pepper, mostly pepper, but it seemed as thick as ever and was longish, wavy, brushing his collar. He and his son sat on a porch step, leaning toward each other with big, matching grins. Two young boys and a pretty, dark-haired woman sat on the step below them laughing at the camera, as if someone had just told a great joke. There were laugh lines around Patrick's eyes and mouth. He wore jeans and a T-shirt with the sleeves rolled up and a cigarette in his hand. *He still smokes.* I had forgotten how much we both smoked back then.

He looked solid and weathered and ruggedly handsome. I thought if I saw him on the street today I would turn to study him appreciatively. He didn't look like the boy I'd known but he'd turned into a fine-looking man.

I wrote his phone number on a Post-It thinking I might call him this evening, and took it with me to the kitchen to make myself some dinner.

I felt happy as I put together a chopped salad with bib lettuce, arugula, spinach, hard-boiled eggs, red onion, artichoke hearts, raisins and sunflower seeds. I kept thinking about Patrick's email and his picture. The familiarity of him felt good and comfortable.

I was checking a loaf of Asiago cheese bread warming in the oven when I heard a key in the front door. My heart skipped a beat and the oven door slammed shut before I realized it wasn't a burglar, it was Michael. The fear dissolved and exasperation replaced it. What was he doing here now?

"Lib," he called.

"In here," I said and heard him drop keys on the table by the front door. Something else dropped as well, probably an overnight bag, and the sound made me furious.

"Mmmm, looks good," he said, kissing me.

"What are you doing here?"

He looked startled. "Nice welcome for your fiancé," he said.

"You never come over on Sunday night. You could have at least called."

"I did. I left you a message."

I hadn't checked voice mail all day. I looked over at the answering machine sitting on the desk in the corner, a big red numeral "one" blinked at me.

"Well, so what's the occasion?" I asked, making an effort to keep my tone even.

"I just wanted to spend the evening with you. I think we should get used to spending more time together, don't you?"

"Michael, you can't just change things because you think we should. We need to talk about it together, make decisions together. I have things to do tonight. I have work to do. I wasn't planning on you being here."

"Well, shit, Lib, you can do your work," he said. "I don't expect us to be together every second. When we're married we're going to have our own things to do."

Thank god for that, I thought. "Tonight doesn't work for me," I said.

"I'll just sit in the living room and watch TV. You won't even know I'm here."

"I'll know you're here," I said, louder than I meant to. "It doesn't work for me, Michael."

He studied me. "So what you're saying is you want me to go home, is that it?"

"*Yes!*"

Silence. Michael swallowed. He looked out the window. Jiggled the change in his pocket. "Fine," he said and turned to go. But then paused in front of the Post-It on the counter. "Who's Patrick?" he said, turning around, thrusting it toward me.

Oh shit. "No one," I said. "A friend. "

"A friend?" he said. "I've never heard you mention anyone named Patrick."

So what, I wanted to shout. He puts a ring on my finger and now I have no life of my own? I have to divulge every aspect of my life, every thought, every person I talk to? But I took a breath and contained myself, kept my voice even.

"He's someone I knew in high school. He lives in Florida. He got in touch with me and we've emailed a couple of times."

"How'd he get in touch with you?"

"Oh for Christ's sake, what's with the interrogation?" Michael's eyes flashed. "He found me on SearchForSchoolmates.com," I said. "You know, that Internet website where you find people from high school."

"When did he do that?"

"All right, that's enough with the twenty questions. You're making a big deal out of nothing."

Michael's gaze bore into my soul, making me feel guilty, as if I'd done something horrible.

"Jesus, Libby," he said, taking off his glasses and rubbing the bridge of his nose. "It doesn't feel like nothing to me. It feels a little coincidental, actually, that you've been emailing some guy from high school and now you're having second thoughts about our engagement. Does that strike you as odd? Because it does me. What would you think if you were me?" He looked at me, challenging me to dispute this. I could see how it looked to him; deceitful and sneaky. But right then I didn't care.

"You're blowing this up out of proportion, Michael. One has nothing to do with the other."

"Then why don't you just explain one and then the other," he said and sat down at the table, arms folded across his chest.

Ten

"Well?" Michael said.

I bristled. "Well what?" All I needed was a spotlight shining down on me to complete the atmosphere.

"Tell me about this Patrick person. Tell me what's going on with him. Tell me what's going on with us. Tell me why it was so terrible that I announced our engagement. Tell me why you're upset that I came over today. Take your pick of topics."

"I don't appreciate your attitude, Michael." He stared. "Nothing's going on with Patrick. Nothing. He's someone I knew in high school who got in touch with me." All right, so I got in touch with him but I wasn't compelled to set that record straight. "We've emailed a few times. End of story."

He didn't look as if he believed me. I could see, though, that he wanted to, that he just needed to hear the right words. "Okay, so what's going on with us?" he said.

"I don't know." Those weren't the right words, I knew.

Michael shook his head and looked at his hands. "Are we engaged or not?"

"I don't know."

His face darkened. His eyes flashed. I thought he was going to pick something up and throw it (nothing dangerous, that wouldn't be Michael) but then he just slumped forward. "What do you mean you don't know? Either we are or we're not."

"You've been making all these decisions about us as if you're the only one in this relationship. I feel out of control, Michael. You decide we're going to get married. You decide when it's time to tell everyone. You decide we need to spend more time together. These are life-changing decisions. These are things we should decide together."

He got up and got a glass of water, drank it down and set the glass down in the sink with a loud clink. It was all I could do not to run over to see if he'd broken one of my good glasses but I held myself back. He stood at the sink, his back rigid.

"Maybe you need a break from me," he said turning around. He ran his hand over his head then thrust his hands in his pocket.

A *break*. It sounded so good to me, I practically swooned with the relief it would bring. But I didn't want to appear eager. "What do you mean?"

"Maybe you need time away from me to figure out what you want, if you want to marry me. Decide if you want your email boyfriend or me."

"Oh, Michael."

"What? How am I supposed to feel? It feels like you're hiding something and I don't like it. I don't like any of it."

"I'm not hiding anything," I said. Was I?

"Maybe, maybe not. But something's going on with you and I don't know what it is. I don't even know any more how you feel about me."

"I don't know how I feel about anything."

"Great."

"It's all just overwhelming to me, Michael. Can you try to see it from my point of view?" He apparently thought that was a rhetorical question. "I'm sorry," I said. "I know how you must feel but there've been too many decisions made, too many changes."

"I don't know what you want from me, Libby." He turned and walked away. I followed him. He picked up his overnight bag and his keys. "I'm going home," he said. "When you figure out what you want, call me." He opened the door.

What did this mean? "Will I see you Wednesday?"

"No," he said over his shoulder.

"Michael," I said.

He wheeled around. *"What, Libby? What?* I asked you to marry me and you said yes and now you don't know if you want to anymore. What does that tell me? I love you but I need to be loved back." He looked at me and I opened my mouth to speak but he put his hand up like a traffic cop.

"I'm done for tonight. I have nothing else to say. I'm going home." And he walked out, shutting the door quietly behind him.

What did I just do? Was he breaking up with me? Is there anything that makes you want someone more than when they don't want you any more? It made me feel weepy and remorseful.

But he was clearly giving me an ultimatum; marry him or else, and I didn't want him to leave not knowing what would happen to us but I couldn't bring myself to run out and stop him now. I couldn't say I was going to marry him. Not now. And nothing else was going to satisfy him.

I looked around the house, at the order, the stillness. Was this what I wanted? To live in my perfect little house, alone? I walked from room to room in the solitude, knowing there would be no one there except Rufus, no sounds that Rufus or I did not make.

I ate a few bites of salad and then I cleaned up the kitchen, washing dishes slowly in soapy water instead of putting them in the dishwasher. I dried them and placed them carefully in the cupboard and wiped the counter tops until they gleamed, moving the offending Post-It as I worked. I straightened the junk drawer, tossing out nails, paperclips and little black rubber things I didn't recognize. Then I went into the living room, straightened the pillows on the sofa and put the newspapers in a basket by the window.

Everything was in order. It was very quiet. I turned on the stereo and put on a Nickleback CD. Michael only listened to oldies and classical music. I turned it up loud. I'd been alone for many years before Michael, and there had been long stretches when there was no man in my life at all, but now it seemed like such a long time ago. I tried to remember how it had been. Mostly, I thought I'd been happy, enjoying the freedom of being single, not having to consider anyone else in my plans, sitting on the couch eating taco chips and salsa for dinner if I wanted, watching old movies instead of sports. But I could remember times when I had felt so lonely I'd go to the mall and walk around just to be with people.

I suddenly felt sad and lonely in my house. Was this how it would be for the rest of my life? Just me and Rufus in my tidy little bungalow? I'd already been married twice; two failures. If I let Michael go now what were the chances I'd find someone to share my life with? Hadn't I used up my share of love vouchers?

Eleven

I tried reading, watched a little TV, went for a walk. And then I came back, retrieved the Post-It and looked at Patrick's number. I turned it over, upside down, waved it around, as if it were a birthday present I was savoring opening. Should I? Well, I did. I dialed the number. It rang once and then again as I tapped my fingernail, rat-a-tat-tat, on the desk. Suddenly I got cold feet and was about to slam down the receiver when a voice said, "Hello?" His voice. I recognized it immediately and blood rushed to my face.

"Hello?" he said again.

"Patrick?"

'Yes...?" He paused. "Libby?"

How'd he know?

"Oh, Libby," he exclaimed, "is that you?"

"It is."

"I'm so happy to hear your voice. Man, this is weird isn't it?" He laughed, a genial, familiar sound, even after thirty-two years. I could see the big smile on his face, but it was the face I last saw, thirty-some years ago, not the new one in the picture he'd sent.

"It's very weird. You sound so much like yourself. It takes me back in time."

"Me too," he said. "Little Libby Carson. Wow. Cool. So how are things?"

"Awful," I said and wanted to grab the word and stuff it right back in my mouth. Couldn't I have made a little small talk first?

"What's going on?" he said, his concern reaching, like a hug, across the wires.

"Michael and I are fighting about this engagement thing. He sort of stormed out earlier."

"What are you fighting about?" he asked.

"Thing is, I'm not sure I want to get married, it was never in my game plan, so of course Michael's not very happy with me right now." What possessed me to tell him this? He'd sounded delighted to hear from me, probably thinking this was going to be a lighthearted "remember-when" kind of conversation, and here I was spilling my guts like a kid in confession.

Watch him hang up on me.

"Wow. Well...oh man, Libby, I'm sorry," he said. What else could he say? I wished I could take it all back, hang up and start over. Why wasn't there a replay button in life? "Are you okay?" he asked.

"I'm okay," I said. "Jeez, I haven't talked to you in thirty-two years and the first thing I do is tell you all my problems."

"It's okay, not to worry," he said. "I'm not so good with my own problems but I'm dynamite with other people's." I chuckled with the relief his words brought. "What are you going to do?" he asked.

Appallingly, tears came then and I couldn't speak except for small embarrassing mewing sounds.

"Libby?"

"Yes," I said in a high-pitched, whiny, cry-baby voice. It was so incredibly embarrassing. I was fifty, for god's sake, not twelve.

"It'll be okay," Patrick said. "It's hard, but you'll work it out."

"Yeah, I know," I said after regaining a scrap of composure. "I'm sorry to be dumping this on you after all these years, to be crying like a baby..."

"Libby," he interrupted, "don't worry about it okay? I love other people's misery. It makes me feel superior and I have so few chances to do that." It felt good to laugh out loud. "Look," he said, "if you want to talk I can listen. If you're not comfortable talking about it to me, that's something else, but if you are then don't worry about it. Talk all you want. We're friends."

"We haven't seen each other in a lifetime."

"Well, so we took a hiatus."

"Tell me about you," I said. "What's going on in your world?"

Patrick talked. I smiled as I listened to the familiar sound of his voice, feeling like I was seventeen again, back in my lavender bedroom with Eric Clapton and David Bowie posters on the walls, idly chattering, making plans to meet before homeroom.

He told me about a kayak tour he did yesterday. "Most tours take about four hours," he said, "but this one took six and a half. Everything that could go wrong, did. There's a name for that, isn't there? What's that called?"

"Murphy's Law," I said.

"Yeah, that's it. I'm renaming it Harrison's Law," he said. "I was already paddling the nine year old son when the father got a cramp and decided to walk back so I had to tow his kayak in. Then when we got back the mom didn't feel well and I'm helping her out of her kayak when she barfs all over it."

I laughed. "At least she didn't barf all over you."

"Really."

"Here I thought you had such a glamorous profession," I said.

"Yes, very glamorous. Cleaning up vomit."

He told me about the weather in Florida and about where he lived on the beach and his dog named Chewbacca. The sound of his voice was soothing and I was happy just to listen and not have to talk. He told me how his son Ashley was working full time, putting himself through school, and still found time for his wife and two kids. He was studying filmmaking, Patrick told me. "There's not a big call for filmmakers in South Florida," he said, "but what the hell. It's his life and he'll figure it out. He's a good kid with a good head on his shoulders in spite of the handicap of being raised by me."

What if Patrick and I had stayed together and gotten married? Ashley could have been our son. Surely we wouldn't have named him Ashley, though.

"You must have done something right," I said.

"All I did was enjoy the hell out of raising him."

"How did you end up raising him?"

"His mom got into drugs when he was little so I took him. By the time she got it together he was settled in with me and things were going pretty well so we left it that way."

"Do they have a good relationship? Your son and his mom?"

"Yeah, now they do. She cleaned up her act after a while. She's doing ok, now."

"Did she ever try to get custody?"

"No. She moved close though and spent as much time with him as she could. We were friends by that time and we worked it out between us."

"How civilized," I said, thinking of the broken relationships in my wake and the fact that I'd never spoken to any of them ever again.

"Yeah, I guess it is. But life's too short to hold grudges."

"God, you're so reasonable. Were you always like that?" I didn't remember this but we were practically children when we were together. I liked his light-heartedness, his easy optimism. It was so different from what I was used to.

"I guess," he said. "I'm not saying we control how we feel but I think we do have choices about how we let what we feel control our lives." He paused. "I should shut up shouldn't I?"

"Not at all. It's a great attitude. How'd you get to be so mentally healthy?"

"Years of therapy," he said. "Hey, I sent you a photo. Did you get it or are you just ignoring it out of respect for my feelings?"

I laughed. "I did. I love it. Your son looks just like you used to."

"And I don't."

"Well, who does? You look great, though. At least in the picture." He laughed. "And your family's very handsome."

"Send me one of you, okay?"

"I will."

I had a fine, cozy feeling as I hung up, glad I'd called. His perspective on life made me feel more philosophical about Michael. Maybe a separation would be good for us. Maybe a little distance would help us realize how important our relationship was. "You'll work this out," Patrick had said and I knew that was true, one way or another. Maybe we'd get married after all, maybe we wouldn't. Maybe I would end up with Patrick instead. I laughed at this silly fantasy, but imagined seeing him again after all these years, gazing longingly into each others' eyes, devouring each others' faces and then hugging excitedly, and professing our long lost love.

Silly stuff. The stuff of romance novels.

Immediately I went to my computer and searched through pictures I had stored on my hard drive. There was one from last year's vacation but I wore a blue dress with a large print that made me look chunky. What was I thinking when I bought that? I made a mental note to get rid of it. There was another that wasn't bad but my neck looked saggy. Then I found one taken at a backyard party at Sophie and Pete's. I was lying on the grass, leaning on my elbow as I played with their small, blonde grandchild. We had both looked up, surprised, when Michael called to me and snapped the picture. Sun glinted off the gray in my hair making it look like shiny highlights and I had an open, unselfconscious smile. I was wearing shorts and a low-cut top, and my legs looked long and sleek, even though they're not all that long. Or all that sleek. But the angle was just right.

Patrick,
It was so much fun talking to you. A blast
from the past.
So here's a picture. Last time you saw me I
wore black eyeliner and had long
straightened hair parted down the middle.
There are a few other changes as well. Hah!

I'm also sending a picture of Sophie and Pete.
Say, didn't you have a big, old black Ford with huge fins that we used to go "parking" in?
Do you have a girlfriend?
Libby

A reply came back within minutes.

Girl, the years have treated you well! Are you sure you didn't hire a stand-in?
I laughed out loud.
No, really, you are still beautiful even without the eyeliner.
Thanks for the picture of S & P. It's great to see them! Give me their email address, would you? I'd love to contact them.
That was a '61 Ford to be specific. I'm flashing back right now. Didn't we used to go to a little covered bridge that was in a housing development somewhere and park there? So neat to pull up these memories.
Peace,
Patrick
P.S. Nope. No girlfriend.
    Good.

Twelve

I didn't talk to Michael on Monday. Or Tuesday. I didn't talk to Michael for almost a week. I didn't call him. I thought about it. I picked up the phone several times but each time I decided I wasn't going to be the one to call. Childish, I know. Sometimes it's hard to believe I'm fifty when I do things like that. But I've found out that things just don't change all that much as you get older. Inside I feel the way I always did. The feelings, the insecurities, the pride are all the same. When you're young you think being middle-aged means you act like an adult. What you don't know until you get here is that in certain things, particularly where love is concerned, we never grow up.

I was ambivalent about my alone-ness. But Rufus loved it. He was happy to have me to himself. Especially at bedtime. When Michael was over there wasn't much room for Rufus, who liked to curl up at my side with a paw resting on my hip. When Michael was there he had to move over to the other side of the bed and didn't appreciate the change. He'd walk around for a while, he'd stand on me looking at Michael, then finally paw around in a new spot and settle in. At some point during the night he'd stalk off.

Now, he was content.

It seemed odd and empty not to see Michael on Wednesday, not to talk to him. I vacillated between relief and anger, loneliness and tranquility, righteousness and rejection. But I survived. At first I was sad, then I got pissed that he didn't call, that he could just turn away because things hadn't gone his way. Fuck him, I thought. Two could play this childish game. I knew I was acting like a spoiled brat but didn't seem able to help myself.

* * *

Dominick was at Mrs. Rosatti's when I arrived for our appointment. "Well, here's the engaged lady," he said. Inwardly I rolled my eyes. "Come join us for tea and coffeecake."

Bea was jazzy in a teal blue pantsuit with splashes of bright white flowers. She wore a chunky white necklace with large hoop earrings. She looked like she should be walking down Collins Avenue in Miami Beach. Dominick's shiny bald head was fringed with fluffy white hair. He was quietly dapper, the antithesis to Bea's in-your-face fashion style. Today he wore a gray cashmere cardigan over a snowy white shirt and navy trousers. This relationship was of the "opposites attract" variety.

Bea put a translucent green glass dish with a humongous piece of pastry in front of me and poured hot water into a matching cup. I don't particularly like tea but to be sociable I picked blackberry from the selection she offered. At first I didn't notice they were hardly speaking to each other, that each of them was addressing their remarks only to me, commenting on the weather, talking about my surprise party. When it finally dawned on me that there was tension in the room I looked up, surprised, first at one, then the other. They were concentrating resolutely on their coffeecake. Bea asked Dominick if he wanted more tea. He said no. She gave him a pointed look and glanced at me.

"Well," he said, suddenly cheerful, "I'd best be on my way. I'll leave you two to your girl's stuff." He kissed Bea on the cheek.

"I'll speak to you later, dear," she said.

When he'd gone I said, "Is everything all right?"

"Oh yes," she said, clearly lying.

"There was a bit of tension in here."

"Oh, I suppose there was," Bea said. "That was rude. We should have been more discreet with our little tiff."

"You were fine," I said. "What are you "tiff-ing" about?" I didn't want to think of people in their seventies having a lover's quarrel. Isn't there a statute of limitations on that kind of bullshit?

"Would you like more tea?" she asked, getting up and putting the fire under the teakettle. "Or how about a sherry?"

"Nothing, thanks," I said. "Come sit down." She turned off the fire and sat. "So tell me," I said.

"Dominick wants us to move in together and I'm not sure it's a good idea. So he's upset."

"Wow," I said amazed at our parallel universes. "It's the same old crap no matter how old you get, isn't it?" She smiled. "Why isn't it a good idea?"

"I've been alone for a long time and I've gotten used to doing things my own way. I don't know that I want to change that. We have such a lovely relationship but I think part of it is that we don't live together so we don't deal with each other every minute. And at our age, what's the point?"

"What does age have to do with it? You always tell me you're only as old as you feel."

"Ah, throwing my words back in my face, eh?"

"Absolutely. You're using age as an excuse."

"I think I was taken by surprise, if you want to know the truth. It never seemed important to Dominick before so I just never thought about it."

"Do you think it would work?"

"I suppose I'll have to think about that now, won't I? How are you handling it? You and Michael don't live together and now you're getting married. How do you think that will work?"

"The $64,000 question," I said. "I have no idea."

"Sounds like this is the time for the sherry," Bea said and poured two glasses. "So, tell me," she said when she sat.

"Looks like we're sort of in the same boat," I said and told her everything that had happened from the proposal to the party to when Michael walked out.

"I don't know Michael well," she said. "He seems like a nice man but if you're not sure you want to get married then, for heaven's sake, don't do it. Make your decision for yourself not for him."

"I don't want to hurt him."

"Is that a good reason to get married? Sometimes people get hurt when you have different ideas of what you want from a relationship. You can't control that. The only thing you can control is you. If you marry him because you don't want to hurt him you'll both be sorry."

Simple, logical, sensible advice. She made it sound so easy.

Bea drained her glass and cleared the table. "Come," she said, "let me show you all the new clothes I bought, all of which need altering, of course."

"What's the occasion," I asked, nearly blinded by the array of colors and patterns she displayed before me. There were several summery pants outfits, one with a pattern like an EKG readout in tangerine and green, a pair of electric blue Capri pants and a violet evening gown with sequins top to bottom.

"We're going on a cruise to the Caribbean," she said, her eyes sparkling.

"How lovely. Maybe spending so much time together will help you decide if you want to live with him," I said.

"It can't hurt," she said.

"Maybe Michael and I should go with you!"

"Come on," Bea said, "you can borrow my clothes!"

Thirteen

I met my sister Jill at Lily's Restaurant a few days later for a belated birthday lunch. She was already seated at a table in a corner in front of a huge potted palm looking elegant and put-together. When Jill was little she was like "Pig Pen" from the *Peanuts* comic strip, clouds of dust always seeming to waft around her. She never really wanted to play paper dolls with me (my favorite thing to do when I was a kid, always the little fashionista) but she did because she wanted to please me; she didn't care about clothes or what she looked like and didn't care what other people thought about her, as long as she had me. We were different but we were pretty inseparable back then and I thought she was such a cute and funny little person.

And then, sometime around ninth grade she did a complete 180. It was amazing, really. She met Mark, now her husband, and next thing I knew she started experimenting with makeup and asking my advice on fashion, even borrowing my clothes which annoyed me no end. It was as if she was a whole new person and I had a hard time relating to her then. Jealousy was part of it but I didn't want her to change because of him, and she didn't need me any more. She and Mark went steady all through high school and college and then got married and started a family. She never even went out with anyone else. And after they got together we were never as close as we'd been before. She didn't need me any more.

I could still see the messy little tomboy she used to be but it was almost as if that was another sister. Now there was no remnant of that person. Now she wore black trousers with a gold chain-link belt, white silk blouse and gold hoop earrings. Her chin-length hair was perfectly highlighted and she brushed her shiny thick bangs off her forehead with a manicured forefinger. I was fashionable, after all it was my business, but much more casual in jeans tucked into knee-high boots and a rather low-cut red top, my frizzy hair pulled back with a ribbon and little corkscrew curls popping out all over the place.

"You look terrific," I told Jill. "Going somewhere this afternoon?"

"My bridge club." Or Junior League or the PTA or the volunteer work she did at the library. Jill always had a millions things going on.

The waiter came by, a twenty-something with dark hair gelled and spiked, blue eyes and a bright white smile. He was obsequious but flirtatious, a good combination for someone hoping to score a big tip from the two older ladies. When I asked how the Caesar salad was and he told me it was good (they put anchovies on top which a lot of restaurants didn't do) but if I wanted the best thing on the menu I should order the Portobello mushroom sandwich. So I did because he made it sound so damn good. Jill ordered an omelet and we both ordered a glass of wine.

"So," Jill said when he'd gone to place our order, "why didn't you tell me Michael proposed?" She wore an expression of challenge as if I always told her everything that went on in my life.

"I didn't have time. He sprung that ring on me and then he sprung the news on everyone at that stupid surprise party, it was crazy."

"He was pretty excited about that party. He had us all believing you'd be thrilled by it."

"I'm not sure I like this new Michael," I said. "I thought we were on the same page about things like marriage and living together. And even surprise parties. I mean, he sort of blindsided me with that ring." I told her how he'd proposed at the restaurant and then about our fight. "I haven't talked to him in days, and we usually talk at least once a day. He's pouting, I think."

"Why don't you call him?" she said.

The waiter brought our wine. "Everything okay here?" he asked.

It would be, I thought, if I wasn't fifty and if I wasn't engaged. "Perfect," I said and he rewarded me with a big, toothy smile. "Your lunch will be ready in a few minutes," he said.

"He likes you," Jill said as he walked away.

"I could be his mother," I said but secretly I was pleased.

"Do you think you're having a midlife crisis?" Jill asked.

"Oh, fuck you," I said and she laughed.

"Being fifty sucks, doesn't it?" she said.

"More than you know. Just wait. You'll see."

"Seriously, though, I think you should call Michael. Don't let this fester."

"He can call me too, you know."

"Lib, don't stand on ceremony here. This is the rest of your life you're talking about. Michael's the best guy you've ever been with. Don't let that go."

The waiter brought our food then and I didn't have to answer but I resented that Jill was siding with Michael. She was my sister, after all, wasn't she supposed to be on my side?

I took a bite of my Portobello sandwich which was delicious but now I didn't feel hungry. Jill took one of my French fries. "You've had some bad luck with men in the past but Michael's someone you can grow old with," she said.

I could see Michael and me sitting in matching easy chairs in a nursing home somewhere, wiping drool off each others' chins. But I couldn't see what led up to it. I couldn't see us married and living together. "Maybe to you he's the best guy I've ever been with but I'm not so sure. Our relationship is fine. It's nice," I said. "It's easy. It's comfortable. But is that reason enough to marry him? Shouldn't it be more…thrilling, more passionate?"

"People get married for different reasons," Jill said. "And I think at our age we have different priorities." She took a cheesy bite of her omelet. "I always thought Michael was your Mr. Right. You always seemed happy with him."

"I am happy with him. I'm happy with things the way they are. And I don't think I want to change it. I'm not so sure we would work as a married couple. Sometimes I feel like I'm a different person when I'm with Michael."

"Maybe you are but is that bad?" Jill asked. "You're more settled. That's a good thing."

I took a bite of my sandwich and wiped my mouth, realizing I'd inhaled three-quarters of it without even tasting it. "I don't want to be *settled.*"

"Lib, that's what marriage is all about, at least the good ones. It's about being settled and comfortable with someone, having someone to count on."

"I've got Rufus."

"Rufus has his limitations."

We both laughed even though I wasn't amused. I wanted to be finished with this conversation. I didn't want any more advice from my little sister who had no idea what the real world was like, who lucked-out at fifteen and met her Prince Charming and lived happily ever after.

But Jill wasn't finished. "You've had the passionate, tumultuous relationships and those didn't work."

"Shit happens, Jill. Not everyone is as lucky in love as you. Just because other relationships haven't worked out doesn't mean this one's right. It's been right for a few years but that doesn't make it right for the rest of my life."

Jill wisely kept her mouth shut. Sometimes she knew when to quit. We ate in silence for a bit as I tried to think of some neutral subject. I thought about Patrick but ruled that out as a topic of discussion. I could just hear her if I brought him up. "Don't throw away your life with Michael for some fantasy," she'd say, I was sure.

"Maybe you should try putting out a different vibe into the universe," Jill said. I chuckled thinking it was a joke but she continued. "A vibe of being grateful and happy with what you've got."

"A *vibe into the universe*? Oh, please." The whole conversation made me feel like I had as a kid when my mother would tell me that eating vegetables would make me stronger and give me the energy to run faster when I was trying out for the track team. I hated vegetables and would move them around on my plate or spit them into a napkin when she wasn't looking and when I won an event it was all I could do not to say, "See, I did it without those stupid vegetables."

"So who's in your bridge club?" I asked and Jill was unable to resist talking about her perfect life and her perfect friends.

Did everyone have to have a life like hers? I felt wistful for the messy little girl she once was, the one who looked up to me and envied my life, who thought I was great and who wanted to be just like me.

I finished my wine as Jill talked and signaled the cute waiter for another glass.

Fourteen

The streets were quiet as I ran through my neighborhood, finishing a six mile run. I usually did the same scenic five mile loop through the forest preserve and back but today I felt good, strong, and it was a crisp, clear morning. The houses were well cared for and I liked the order of it all. Here and there someone raked leaves, swept sidewalks, cleaned gutters. I turned onto Cherry Street and almost ran into a tree when I saw a For Sale sign out front of my favorite house. "Unbelievable," I muttered. The house looked inviting with its beautiful porch and white picket fence and I wondered why they were selling. A divorce? A lost job? Or maybe they were empty nesters who were moving to a condo.

I don't believe in signs from above. I don't. But there was the tiniest voice in my brain telling me this meant Michael and I should get married after all and buy this house and live happily ever after. Is that all it would take? The right house? Maybe this was the vibe Jill talked about.

I ignored the little voice.

The light was blinking on the answering machine when I walked in and I wondered if it was finally Michael. His silence was beginning to piss me off. Now it seemed like a stand-off and the one who called first would have to give in.

But it wasn't Michael, it was Patrick, and relief and affection spread through me like warm milk as I listened to his message.

"Hey, I had a great idea," his once-again familiar voice said. "I was thinking I'd come to Chicago and take you to lunch. What do you think? No pressure. No stress. We'll just have lunch and then I'll go home. Doesn't that sound like fun? It would be great to see you."

Come to Chicago for lunch? It was outrageous. But my heart was pounding when the message ended. Was he serious? It was so impulsive, so daring, so extraordinary. So unlike anything that ever happens in my life.

I dialed his number and when he answered I said, "Okay, do I need to remind you that you live a thousand miles away?"

"Hey!" he said, clearly happy to hear from me.

"That's a tough commute for lunch."

"It's not so bad," he said. "Some people spend hours getting to work every day. It's just a quick plane ride." His enthusiasm made me feel young and reckless. "So when should I come? Tomorrow?"

"Oh, god no, not tomorrow for heaven's sake!" I said, feeling and equal measure of elation and terror.

"Just kidding," he said. "How about Friday, though? Would that work for you?" I felt a giggle rising up from my stomach and I looked at my calendar. I had someone coming in for a fitting on Friday and a dentist appointment in the afternoon. The fitting was at 9:00

a.m. The dentist appointment could be rescheduled. But should I tell him that? Should I really going to let him do this?

"Friday could work," I found myself saying.

"Outstanding," Patrick said. "I'll email the details."

After we said goodbye I stood there grinning like a moron, thoughts racing around my brain like ping pong balls. I imagined us eating lunch at the airport amid the hustle and bustle of travelers. Would it be awkward? What would he look like in person? Would we be as comfortable in person as we were on the phone? Should I call my hairdresser and get rid of the gray? Could I lose five pounds by Friday? Should I call a plastic surgeon?

The part of me that wasn't overwhelmed was inflated like a joyous bubble at the thought of seeing Patrick Harrison.

I had to tell Sophie.

"You're kidding," she said, when I called her. "He's coming to Chicago just for lunch? How fun. And decadent. Can Pete and I come?"

"No!" I said.

"He emailed Pete. Pete was really excited to hear from him. He said we should plan a trip to Florida to visit."

"Let's all go," I said. "We'll make it a road trip. Just like that time we all drove to St. Louis? Remember? In our senior year?"

"I remember," Sophie said. "I remember that ratty motel we stayed in."

"Missouri cockroaches are the biggest cockroaches in the world. Patrick went after one with his boot and it got right up and ran away."

"I hate to rain on your parade," Sophie said, "but what about Michael?"

"Michael?"

"Michael."

"Oh god, Sophie, I don't know. It's just lunch. Why do I have to worry about Michael now?"

"Because you're engaged, even if you're not sure you want to be, and you're going to have lunch with your high school sweetheart who's traveling 1200 miles to see you. That's why."

"Oh," I said. "Yeah, there's that."

Fifteen

I'd been sitting at the curb at O'Hare airport for eighteen minutes, watching people briskly filing through the doors of the terminal, looking for someone who resembled the picture of the current-day Patrick. Clusters of people rushed out for a while and I scanned them carefully but then traffic slowed and people trickled out in ones and twos. I pulled down my visor and checked myself in the mirror to make sure there was no lipstick on my teeth, keeping an eye on the terminal doors. I wondered what Patrick would think when he saw me. How did I compare with the me that he knew so many years ago? Would he even recognize me?

A man about the right age walked out and looked up and down the row of waiting cars. My heart thumped as I studied him but unless Patrick had put on fifty pounds since his picture was taken (a possibility that hadn't occurred to me), it wasn't him. I blew out a breath when the man walked away. I glanced in the mirror again; checked my makeup and hair. Several more men came out of the terminal but two of them were too young and the third was a large black man in a UCLA jacket. I drummed my fingers on the steering wheel and fluffed the hair at the back of my neck.

A tall distinguished man in a trench coat walked quickly out to the curb as a beautiful woman got out of the Mercedes in front of me. They embraced and kissed tenderly. He pulled back, looked deeply into her eyes, and broke into a wide grin. I smiled as the woman put her hand on his cheek. She was elegantly dressed in a long charcoal-gray coat over an ivory turtleneck. I wished I looked as lovely. After all the clothes I'd tried on I'd settled on tan pleated trousers with a cream-colored sweater and short tweed jacket. Was it too dressy? Did it look like I was trying too hard? Maybe my chunky gold necklace was too much, I thought, examining it in the mirror. I took it off and threw it in my purse.

I'd worked late into last night, too keyed up to sleep. I'd finished altering two pairs of pants and ripped apart a jacket before feeling tired enough to go to bed. And then I'd fallen asleep at once only to awaken an hour later. It was worse than high school.

And all night Michael's face would rise up in my mind and his disappointment and hurt at what I was doing. What if he found out? What if he just happened to be meeting a friend at the airport at exactly the same time and we ran into each other and he saw me with Patrick?

A man and woman came out of the terminal and stood chatting animatedly at the door. The woman was plump and wore a long black cape. She had tight silver curls and threw her head back to laugh, the breath floating from her mouth in a plume. He wore a turtleneck and sport coat but no overcoat. Then they shook hands and the woman walked toward the taxi stand. The man stood for a moment looking around. My breath quickened as he started for my car, smiling. In the few seconds before I opened my door to get out I saw that this new Patrick was quite different from the boy of eighteen with long dark hair and black leather. His hair was still on the long side, not quite reaching his collar, and was more gray than brown. His face was fuller and his body heavier, but thankfully not by fifty pounds. He wore no leather, no chains, just that big smile and shining eyes. I swallowed hard.

He grinned when I walked around the car to the passenger side and we stood looking at each other. There he was, Patrick of old, but softer, less angular, more cozy-looking. His eyes had faint creases in the corners.

Sophie would be saying, "Look at him, Libby. Just *look* at him. He's gorgeous."

He studied my face, looking into my eyes, at my hair, my mouth. "Unbelievable," he said and we laughed.

"Good unbelievable or bad unbelievable," I asked even though the answer was painted clearly in his eyes. And that made us laugh even more. We couldn't seem to stop laughing and people turned to look at us, chuckling. Patrick opened his arms and I folded into him, wrapping my arms around his substantial fifty-something body. He held me for a moment, kissed me on the cheek, pulled back and looked deeply into my eyes. He smiled. Just like the guy with the Mercedes woman. I was completely charmed. I felt like I had in high school the first time he asked me out. I could see his admiration back then too and it had puffed me up with pleasure.

We decided to drive downtown and take a walk before finding someplace for lunch. "Aren't you cold?" I asked as we walked north on the lakefront path.

"Not bad," he said. "Why? Are you?"

"No, I'm fine. See this thing I'm wearing? It's called a coat. It's a great little invention."

"I got rid of mine when I moved to Florida and swore I'd never buy another," Patrick said. "I turned the house upside down looking for this turtleneck."

"When we were in high school you always wore black turtlenecks, do you remember?" I asked.

"I think we both always wore them."

"I wore them because you did and you looked so cool and I wanted to be cool too."

He laughed and put his arm around me for a second and I had to work at keeping a big, dopey grin off my face. He hugged me to him quickly and then let me go. No, I thought, don't let go.

Our conversation was light and casual, and there was no mention of Michael, thank god. I kept sneaking looks at Patrick, getting used to how he looked now. The boy I knew was in there; he moved with the same familiar, relaxed grace and his eyes wrinkled up at the corners when he smiled.

We talked about his flight, security at the airport, the weather in Chicago, the weather in Florida. We talked about the traffic on the Kennedy Expressway on the way into town. We filled an awkward silence with a discussion about the temperature of Lake Michigan and how calm it was today. Patrick seemed more recognizable as we walked, his gestures, his expressions, his smile.

"Hungry?" I asked.

"Starved," he said.

The Cheesecake Factory was packed with Michigan Avenue shoppers and tourists and we were told there would be a forty-five minute wait for a table.

"Want to go somewhere else?" I asked.

"No, I'm fine with waiting," Patrick said. "It's part of the Chicago experience. Where I live you can walk into any restaurant, sit right down, order and eat, including dessert and coffee, in about half an hour."

We went to the bar and Patrick ordered Bloody Marys.

"Do you like small town living?"

"Yeah, I do," he said. "I like knowing everyone. I like how simple it is. It's a different life, that's for sure." Very different from my own life.

When the bartender brought our drinks we clicked glasses and drank to our reunion.

"You look even better in person," Patrick said. "You're definitely aging gracefully. And I like the gray in your hair. It looks great."

I flushed with his compliment. "Thanks," I said. "I considered coloring it this morning before you got here but ran out of time."

"I'm glad," he said. "So bring me up to date on the last thirty-two years."

I gave him the Cliff Notes about my college years, my two marriages and my mid-life career change. I told him about some of my clients, about Sophie and Pete and their girls. He told me about his ex-wife, how he got started in the kayaking business, how he'd taught his son to fish and play guitar. "I told Ashley and his wife about how we reconnected and that I was coming to see you and they got a kick out of it."

"So why don't you have a girlfriend?" I asked

"I don't know. I lived with someone for about five years but that didn't work out."

"When was that?"

"A couple years ago."

"What happened?"

Patrick laughed. "Don't be shy, Libby. Just get right to the point here."

"Sorry," I said, feeling chastened. "You don't have to answer. I'm just curious. Just tell me to shut up."

"I'm kidding," he said and his grin loosened my shoulders. "I don't mind. My life's an open book."

"Okay," I said. "So why didn't it work?"

He laughed again. "We just had different interests. At first it didn't seem to matter but after a while it got to be a problem. She was ambitious, a corporate hot shot. I don't think I was the right image for her. Not that she ever said that," he said. "She was really sweet but our relationship just sort of fizzled out."

"Do you date much?"

"Haven't recently," he said. I was pleased.

When the hostess came by to tell us our table was ready Patrick said, "Saved by the bell," and put his hand gently on my back as we followed her to our table. She smiled prettily at him as she handed him a menu. Her shiny blonde hair hung in a satiny spill to her waist and she wore a cropped top and tight black hip-hugger bell-bottoms.

"Didn't you used to have an outfit like that?" Patrick asked.

As we shared a piece of turtle cheesecake for dessert I thought how easy it was to be with him. It didn't feel awkward, there were no uncomfortable silences, it was almost as if no time had passed at all.

"I always thought you were pretty, Libby, but you're even prettier now. Your face has more character."

"Character is just a euphemism for wrinkles," I said.

"Wrinkles mean life. They tell a story. I think faces are so much more interesting when we get older."

"I think faces are so much older when we get older."

His face and arms were browned from the sun. He had a familiar small chip in a front tooth that was so endearing. I wasn't sure if he was really handsome or if I was simply reacting to our history but I liked looking at him.

He leaned forward and took my hand. "I'm really glad you emailed me," he said.

"Me too," I said. "I was so happy that you remembered me."

"Oh Libby, how could I not remember you? Unless I'd been in a coma. I have to say it's great seeing you after all these years." He picked up his glass. "To reunions," he said and we sipped our drinks. The whole thing seemed like a dream.

Then Patrick asked, "How are things with Michael?" crashing like a steamroller through the fog of my trance.

"Ooh, a dose of reality," I said. I took a tiny bite of cheesecake. "Frankly, I feel a little guilty being here with you. That's how things are with Michael."

"I'm sorry," he said. "Not sorry because you're here with me, sorry you're feeling guilty. I want you to enjoy this reunion."

"I am. Very much. That's why I'm feeling guilty, I guess."

"I suppose that's a good sign then. For me, anyway." He grinned, that sweet recognizable grin. I was glad he didn't ask any more about Michael. I didn't really want to think about him right now.

After lunch we walked down Michigan Avenue and looked in the store windows. Patrick pointed out things he thought I'd look good in and mostly they were things I'd pick out for myself. Except for the slinky, low-cut black sequined dress with spaghetti straps and a thigh-revealing slit.

"Thirty years ago, maybe," I said. "Not today."

"You could pull it off," he said. I couldn't. But I loved that he thought I could.

We bought caramel corn at Garrett's and munched on it as we made our way down to the Chicago River and on over to State Street. We went into Macy's and Patrick lamented the fact that it was no longer Marshall Field's. "My mom used to bring all us kids down here when we were little to see the Christmas windows and eat in the Walnut Room."

"They still do the windows."

"Not the same," he said and I agreed.

We wandered through the men's department where Patrick picked up a package of jockey shorts and some socks.

"What? They don't have underwear in Florida?"

He smiled "Let's go find me another turtleneck," he said

I stopped. "Patrick. What are you doing?"

He faced me with a mischievous smile and a twinkle in his eye. "I was thinking I'd stay the night just on the off-chance I could see you again tomorrow."

My heart thumped against my rib cage. My mouth went dry. I was thrilled. And panicked. "You said lunch. You said we'd have lunch and then you'd leave. You promised."

He put his hand on my shoulder. "I'm scaring you, aren't I?" I nodded. "I'm sorry. I don't want to cause trouble. Look. I'll put these back." He turned around and put the socks on a rack. The black socks on top of white ones. I resisted the urge to put them in the right place. "If you want me to go I'll go. I promised and I meant it. I will. But I don't want to. I don't want to leave you yet."

"It's not that I want you to go," I said. "It's just that…"

"Look, I'll stay one night. I don't have to get back for anything so it's no big deal for me. So I'll just stay. We'll talk tomorrow. And then if you want me to go home, I'll go. I promise."

"I've heard *that* before," I said.

He smiled. "Yeah, I know. Another promise. But I mean it. No pressure. I swear, if you don't want to see me tomorrow I'll go home. You don't even have to call me. If I don't hear from you by noon I'll leave. And no hurt feelings." He put his hand on my shoulder again. "What do you say? It's your call."

Why not? All I had to do was not call him tomorrow and he'd be gone. I had the whole rest of the evening and all night to think about it. Not that there was much doubt in my mind.

I picked up the package of socks and handed them to him. "Let's go find you a turtleneck," I said and he broke into a heartbreakingly adorable, chip-toothed grin.

It was fun walking through the store together, holding hands, looking for all the world as if we were a couple. I was aware of people looking at us and imagined their envy. They were thinking we looked good together. They were thinking how nice that we were still in love after all these years now that our children were grown and gone. They were thinking, *Look at this older couple holding hands. Isn't that sweet?*

Patrick put his arm around me as we walked away from the register and the sales girl smiled at us.

"Have a nice evening," she said brightly as if she knew something.

I pulled up in front of the Palmer House Hotel and a doorman hurried over to open Patrick's door. Patrick put up one finger and turned back to me. "Well, girl," he said, "this has been one ass kickin' kind of day."

I laughed. "That's not exactly how I would have described it but it has definitely been some kind of day."

"Some kind of good?"

"Some kind of good."

He took my hand in his and kissed it. *Kissed it.*

"Libby," he began but then he stopped and shook his head. "Libby, Libby, Libby," he said, leaned over and kissed my lips very softly. He pulled back and looked into my eyes and then he kissed me again, more insistently. And then I kissed him back. With the doorman standing there waiting to open the door.

I remembered this about Patrick: he was a great kisser.

"I'm just not ready to let you go," he said. I wasn't ready either. It was the last thing I wanted to do. "Why don't you let the valet take your car and come have a drink with me?"

I put that car right in *park.* "Lead the way," I said.

As Patrick checked in at reception, I told him I'd wait in the bar while he put his things in the room. "Chicken," he said as I turned and walked away. I turned around and smiled but I kept right on heading to the bar.

He was right. I was chicken. But there was no way I was going to be alone in a room with just him and me and a bed.

Sixteen

"Come here often?" Patrick said, startling me as I sat at the bar sipping a glass of wine. The room was dimly lit and if you didn't know it was 4:00 in the afternoon you'd think it was midnight. There were only two other people at the bar and one person sitting at a table talking on a cell phone and taking notes.

"How's your room?" I asked after Patrick ordered a beer.

"Nice," he said. "Want to see?"

Yes, I wanted to say. "No way."

"Okay, okay," he said. "I'll stop." But I didn't really want him to, I liked the sexual banter. It made me feel sexy and desirable. It made me feel like a teenager.

"Okay, here's the deal," I told him. "I have dinner plans tonight so I have to be out of here no later than six." I didn't have dinner plans. I had no plans at all. But it seemed like a good idea for him to think so. It felt like I could get into trouble so easily. Here I was fifty years old and I was making up a story because I didn't trust myself to be alone with him.

"Great," he said. "We've got almost two hours."

We sipped wine and reminisced about high school. We talked about Sophie and Pete and how great it was that they were still together.

"Remember the senior prom? The four of us going to North Avenue Beach at four in the morning? I still remember the dress you wore."

"You do not," I said.

"It was blue and long and had rhinestone straps. And your shoes matched perfectly. I think they even had something rhinestone on them, didn't they?"

"Are you gay?" I asked, narrowing my eyes at him.

He laughed. "Just a good memory."

"You're amazing. My mom had those shoes dyed to match. And she put rhinestone clip-on earrings on them. I can't believe you remember that."

"I remember everything. I remember how we used to meet at the parking lot before school."

"Me too. I was grounded after New Years so you couldn't pick me up. Do you remember?" He nodded. "So I'd take the bus and meet you in the parking lot."

"Where we'd make out until the bell rang and then we'd run like hell to make it to homeroom."

"My parents never did get to know you."

"They hated my long hair and black leather."

"I wonder what they'd think today."

"They'd probably think my hair was still too long. And that I needed a real job."

When we started our second glass of wine Patrick took my hand. I was feeling the wine, but mostly just drunk with the whole idea of Patrick Harrison here, now, and I giggled.

"What?" he said.

"This is just so strange."

"I know," he said and kissed me, once, and then again. "Like a couple of kids."

"We used to make out in the parking lot at school and here we are, fifty years old, making out at a bar in downtown Chicago," I said.

"We're not exactly making out," he said. "But I'd be happy to oblige." He said this with an exaggerated leer. I felt happy inside, like someone who'd just won a prize.

"People are looking at us," I said.

"Do you care?"

"Not really," I said. And I didn't. Unless someone who knew Michael was here.

For a while we sat silently, sipping our wine. Patrick seemed easy and comfortable. I wished I could jump into his brain and find out what he was thinking. He ran his pinky along the back of my hand. We looked at each other in the mirror over the bar.

"Why'd we break up?" Patrick asked.

"I don't think we did. At least I don't remember any big scene. Do you? You're the one who remembers everything."

"I don't."

"I went away to college. I think that's what happened. We called each other for a while but it was tough being so far away."

"We were stupid. We shouldn't have let it go."

In my head I said, "So, wanna go up to your room?" and off we'd go where we'd ravage each other like sex-crazed maniacs and profess our undying love.

Instead I looked at my watch. "Oh shit. It's 6:30," I said.

"How'd that happen?"

I put on my coat and kissed him. "I've got to go." I felt virtuous about my resolve, all the while imagining us doing wicked things to each other.

He put his arm around me and walked me to the door while I argued with myself in my head about leaving. What would happen if I stayed? Would that be so terrible? What was so great about being virtuous anyway?

"So, I'm not going to call you, remember?" he said. "If you want to see me call me in the morning. Otherwise I'll just head home."

"I remember," I said.

He kissed the top of my head. "So do you think you'll do that?"

Of course.

"You'll just have to wait and see," I said.

When I got home I felt jumpy and keyed-up, but now that I was away from him I was glad I'd left. Now, the few things of Michael's around the house made me brought a fresh, new batch of guilt.

Rufus rubbed himself against my legs and meowed for a treat, which I gave him. And then he wanted to settle into my lap to be petted but I couldn't sit. I put on my running clothes, stretched a little, up on my toes, up and down, up and down. I put my hands against the wall to stretch my calves, pulled each leg up to stretch my quads. And then I went out and did a couple easy laps around the block before heading to the track at the high school and running four nine-minute miles. Which used to be slow for me but now, at fifty, felt like lightning.

There was no way anything could happen with Patrick, after all these years. We were two different people now, had very different lives. It was a nice fantasy but Patrick was a dream, Michael was my reality. Patrick was my past, Michael my present. Patrick couldn't be the answer to whatever was going to happen with Michael. That situation needed to be resolved on its own.

I knew all that. In my head. And I was a logical person. But I felt reckless, animated. I felt like I needed to run ten more miles. At least.

Seventeen

There are few things as jarring as the ringing of a phone in the middle of the night. I jolted awake, my heart racing. When I saw that it was 3:51 a.m. my first reaction was fear. Who would call me at that hour? But then I smiled, sure it was Patrick, and picked up the receiver.

"Couldn't sleep for thinking about me?" I said.

But it wasn't Patrick.

"Libby," my mom said. "Can you come over?"

I sat up, my chest thumping. "Mom, it's four o'clock in the morning."

"I know, honey, I'm sorry."

I was already out of bed, stripping off my pajamas, pulling on underwear "What is it? Are you okay?"

"It's Daddy. Something's wrong." Her voice was filled with confusion, anguish.

My head pounded. I dug my knuckle into my temple. "Did you call 911?" I asked and pulled on jeans, zipping them, looking around for my shoes.

"I didn't know what to do."

Oh god. "I'll call them, Mom. Hang up, okay? I'll call them and then I'll be right there." A small sound escaped her throat. I made my voice calm to hide my impatience. "He'll be okay, Mom," I said, but I didn't feel that optimism in my bones. I walked back and forth in front of the dresser, pounding my thigh with my fist. "Hang up, now. I'll be right there."

My hand shook as I punched in 911 and choked out the address. I knew I had to keep it together for my mother but as I tied my shoes a wail gathered in my throat like a giant ball of peanut butter. *Please, no. Not yet. Let him be all right.*

I wasn't ready. I still needed my father. It didn't matter that I was fifty years old. At that moment I felt ten. Six. Five years old. My dad was my biggest fan. He was my rock. We had a connection that I had with no one else in the world.

What was wrong? I imagined my father lying utterly still in bed. Had he had a stroke? A heart attack? My own heart seized up at the thought.

Daddy.

They were lifting the stretcher down the porch steps to a waiting ambulance as I drove up, lights strobing the neighborhood. My mother was holding my father's hand, running alongside, quick little steps, dressed in her blue chenille bathrobe. He looked fine when I got to him, just sleeping. I touched his cheek. "I love you, Daddy," I whispered, watching for a finger twitch or the tremble of an eyelid. I thought if he were dead they'd be carrying him out completely covered by the sheet and took solace in that.

"I'll be right behind you," I told my mother as the EMT helped her into the back of the ambulance. "I'll get you some clothes." She was oblivious to the fact that she was in her bathrobe and probably wouldn't care even if she did realize it but it was something useful I could do.

There were little clusters of people in the waiting room; a woman with wiry gray hair and three children wearing Chicago Cubs caps, a young couple with black hair, black lipstick, black nail polish and silver posts through their noses. And my mother, sitting alone, looking very small, turned in on herself, hands folded in her lap, head down, fluffy blue slippers on her feet, white hair spiked around her head. I stood in the doorway afraid to talk, afraid to move, just looking at her. I had a bad feeling. How could I comfort her? Who was going to comfort me? She looked up then, tried to smile. I sat beside her, hugged her, patted her hair down, put my hand on hers.

"I called Jill," I said. "She and Mark are on the way."

She nodded.

"I brought you some clothes." I pointed at the paper bag on the floor. She stared where my finger pointed but I could see it wasn't registering. She was oblivious to the fact that she was in her bathrobe.

"Doesn't matter," I said and we sat in silence, Mother's foot tapping softly in her slipper.

"What happened?" I asked.

She slumped forward and put her face in her hands. I rubbed her bony back. "I don't know. He moaned in his sleep. I thought he was dreaming and I went back to sleep." Her voice cracked.

"Shhhh…" I said. "You couldn't know, Mom." She sat back and I put my arm around her. She was trembling.

"But then something woke me. He was so still." Her shoulders shook and tears fell down her cheeks. "I should have done something earlier. If he doesn't make it it's my fault."

"No, Mom. It'll be all right. He'll pull through." What else could I say? I rubbed her shoulder, wishing someone were there to rub mine.

And then, thankfully, Jill and Mark rushed in, Jill in an old sweatshirt and sweatpants, her hair looking like she'd just gotten out of bed, which, of course, she had. Mark was in jeans and a Notre Dame T-shirt. I almost cried with the relief of seeing them. And right behind them was Michael. The sight of his face took my breath away. I was surprised by his presence but glad Jill had called him. He scooped me up in a big, protective hug and I melted into his chest. He smelled like Michael, a clean, sleepy smell.

"You okay?" he asked and I nodded into his chest. He patted my hair and I exhaled. "He'll come out of this, Lib. He's going to be fine." His sureness settled around me like a safety net.

Eighteen

It's not that I didn't think at all about Patrick. I was certainly aware, somewhere in the recesses of my mind, that he'd left town thinking I didn't want to see him. But I couldn't let myself think about Patrick when my father was in a coma caused by a stroke. As I sat by his side I could only think that he might never again hear me tell him I loved him. I might never again feel his arms around me or hear his voice or see his smile. I stayed, holding his hand, talking to him when my mother was sleeping or had gone home to bathe and change clothes. Jill was there too, in and out. She encouraged me to go home, get some rest. "There's nothing you can do here," she told me, but I thought my voice could wake him. I thought if anyone could bring him back, I could. So I kept talking.

"Remember the time you took Jill and me to the Cubs game, Daddy? Remember the bobble-head dolls you bought us? I still have mine." I did. It sat on a shelf in my workroom next to my favorite family photo taken when Jill and I were just toddlers in little ruffled sunsuits.

I watched closely for the slightest tremor, an acknowledgement that he heard. But there was nothing, no movement. He looked small and vacant lying there. So I kept on.

"How about that time I hit a grand slam when I was ten and we won the game and the league championship? Remember that? I know you do. You honked the horn all the way to Baskin-Robbins and bought the biggest sundae they could make with all my favorite flavors and the four of us toasted me on every spoonful. Do you remember? It had butter pecan, chocolate-chocolate-chip, Rocky Road…what else? Did it have turtle ice cream too? It had chocolate sauce, caramel sauce, raspberry. It had everything! And then it had mounds of whipped cream and a cherry on top. Do you remember that, Daddy? It was gross. And we ate the whole thing. I couldn't look at ice cream for a year after that."

I remembered what he'd said after Michael announced our engagement, about not having to worry about me any more so I told him how great Michael had been during this time, how he'd bring me clean clothes, homemade sandwiches, soup in a thermos.

"He never tells me I should go home, Daddy. He knows I need to be here. He comes and goes. Sometimes he sits with me and makes sure I eat something and then he kisses me and leaves and comes back again later. He's been my rock, my anchor. You're right, Dad, you won't have to worry about me after Michael and I are married. He's a good man."

I thought if only he would just wake up now I'd marry Michael tomorrow and he would walk me down the aisle.

Sophie and Tiffany came by. Sophie brought magazines and books. She brought *The Kite Runner* and *To Kill a Mockingbird* but I couldn't concentrate enough to read. She went to my house and made macaroni and cheese, and lasagna, and made sure Rufus's litter box was scooped and that he had food and water. She checked my email and responded to clients for me.

"There was an email from Patrick," she said. The sound of his name shocked me in the hospital setting.

"What did it say?" For a second I was back at the bar at the Palmer House, holding hands with him, giggling together, feeling something sweet and old-new in the pit of my stomach.

"I didn't read it," she said.

I laughed. "You did too."

"No, truly, I didn't. It just didn't feel right. But I had Pete email him later to tell him about your dad. I hope that's okay."

"It's fine," I said. I wanted to read that email. But I thought if I denied myself this pleasure my father might wake up.

And on the third day my father opened his eyes. My mother was sitting in the chair by the window, leafing through an old issue of Better Homes and Gardens. I was sitting by his bed trying to read *The Kite Runner*. Out of the corner of my eye I saw his finger move and my head snapped up. My father was looking at me, his blue eyes soft and confused. I thought he didn't recognize me for a minute and a sharp pain grabbed my chest. But then he said, "Hi pumpkin," and my eyes filled. Oh my god. He was alive. He knew me. He was going to come out of this.

My mother rushed over and took his hand. I touched his arm, his face. Our tears fell on his blanket.

"What happened?" he whispered. "Where…"

I pushed the button for the nurse and my mother told him what had happened. While she talked he closed his eyes and a knife of panic stabbed my heart, but when she stopped talking he opened them again. "Don't cry," he said to me, and then, "Tired…"

A nurse came in and when she saw my father awake she ran out and called out orders to the aides and suddenly the room was alive with activity and we were asked to please wait in the lounge. I argued, not wanting to leave him but she gently led me to the door and asked that they be allowed to do their work.

I called Jill and Michael while we waited. When I told Jill he was awake she made a squeaky, "Ooooohhhhh," sound and could hear that she was choking back tears when she said she was on her way. Michael said, "I'm so glad, Lib. I knew he'd be okay, I just felt it." I was soothed by his words. He, too, said was rushing over. I called Sophie. I wanted them all; my sister, her husband, her kids, Michael, Sophie, Mark. I wanted everyone there with my mom and me when we saw my father again. I wanted him to know how much he was loved so he would fight to stay with us.

We waited, talking quietly, all of us, speculating if Dad would need to go to rehab, what his condition would be, if he'd have any paralysis, if his brain had been affected.

"We'll hope for the best but prepare for the worst," my mother said in her no-nonsense way. "We'll manage whatever we need to manage."

"One of my clients is a physician who doesn't practice any more, now he's a medical consultant," Michael said. "He specializes in elder care and I know he'll be happy to help out. He knows everybody in the industry." Michael smiled tenderly at my mother and she patted his hand. Her fingers shook a little. I put my head on his shoulder.

The doctor came in then, removing his glasses and rubbing the bridge of his nose. He paused a moment, scanned the room and when he spied us he started forward, replacing his glasses. The skin under his eyes was thin as tissue, and pleated with wrinkles. He had a kind face but there was something in his gaze that glued me to my seat. I gripped Michael's knee and held my breath while my mother and Jill bounced up as one, standing hopefully in front of him.

"I'm so sorry, Mrs. Carson," the doctor said.

My mother stared. She put her hand up to her face. Her mouth opened. "What?" she said.

My stomach was a stone inside me. I looked at Michael in disbelief. I'd just seen my father and he looked like he would be all right. How could this be? Tears gathered behind my eyes. *No. No. No.* My breath caught in my throat. I didn't get to tell him I loved him again.

I put my face in my hands. *No. No. No. No. No.*

Nineteen

I was lucky to be fifty years old and to have never lost anyone this close to me. I'd lost an aunt and two uncles and their deaths left me saddened, but losing my father rocked me to my core. If there'd been a devastating illness or a long-term slide into senility it wouldn't have blind-sided me like this. But, whatever, are you ever ready to lose a parent? Are you ever prepared for the hole it will leave in your universe? Losing my father so suddenly, seeing him so healthy and vibrant one day and dead the next, left me shaken and lost and feeling disoriented.

The next few days went by in a stupor of activity; calling friends and family to let them know, making funeral arrangements, running errands, dealing with my mother's grief, and my own and Jill's, and trying to keep up with my work. I couldn't get my head around the concept that my father was gone and tried to keep my mind busy so I wouldn't have to think. Michael called several of my clients to tell them I'd be unavailable for a few days but I did manage to finish all the alterations to

Mrs. Rosatti's cruise clothes. Michael delivered them to her just in time and she called to thank me and express her condolences.

I finally read the email from Patrick.

Lib, it said. **I'm so sorry to hear about your dad. I am praying for him to get well and I'm praying for you to be strong. If there's anything I can do please call me. I know that sounds ridiculous, what could I do after all, but I do mean it, Lib. My thoughts are with you.**
Love,
Patrick

He'd written it before. He didn't know my father was dead. And I couldn't tell him. I couldn't even thank him for his kind words. I know it sounds silly, I know that now, but then it felt like a betrayal to even be reading the email. It felt like a betrayal of my father who believed in my relationship with Michael, it felt like a betrayal of Michael's trust, of course (and he'd been so loving and supportive through this), and it felt like a betrayal of who I was, or thought I should be.

But I wasn't in my right mind.

I stayed at my mother's house the days before the funeral so we'd be able to kiss each other goodnight and see each other's face in the morning. Michael drove me over each night, my mother made steaming mugs of hot chocolate and we talked about my father. She told us stories of when they were first married and Michael and I sat side by side on the couch, holding hands, sipping from our thick green mugs. Then Michael left us for the night and I slept in my old bedroom which still had lavender walls but no longer had the flowered-print, ruffled comforter and pillow shams.

It was a good thing to do, staying there. My mother and I leaned on each other, we helped each other cope and let each other cry. We didn't need to be strong for anyone else, we just alternated it for each other. We remembered vacations and events, family outings and birthdays, anniversaries and graduations. We remembered picnics and dinners and the sweet mundane days of my childhood.

"You girls were the pride of his life," my mother said. She had dark circles under her eyes and her hair was uncharacteristically messy, curls spiraling around her head. "Whenever he took you somewhere people would say, 'Here comes Harry and his girls.' He was so proud of that."

"I wish I'd had what you guys had," I said. "I wish things had worked out with Jason and that we'd had a family. We'd have been married thirty years now. I could be a grandmother."

"It doesn't pay to look back, Libby." I could see that my regret made her sad.

"I know. But I envy what you and dad had. It must give you some comfort now."

My mother poured more chocolate into my mug and added a dollop of whipped cream. "It does, honey. I had fifty-two years with a man I was crazy about." She daintily licked the spoon. "But it wasn't all peaches and cream."

"Well, no relationship is. But you were so in-tune, so…united."

"We were. But don't idealize it, honey. And don't use it as a scale to measure your own success or failure. It was human. Real life."

"Well, of course it was. But it was still an enviable relationship. I want that." I sounded like a pouty little girl.

"Honey, your dad and I were kids when we got married, we grew up together. You and Michael had whole lives before you met. We didn't, really. What we had is strictly ours based on our experience and our history and how we grew together, and what you have with Michael is its own thing and it comes from your separate experiences. You have a lot to merge but you can still grow and learn together."

I thought about her words later as I lay in bed unable to sleep, feeling like a little girl in my childhood bed, wishing to go back to those times for just an hour. I suppose I did compare my life to theirs. I did always think I'd grow up and get married and have a family and duplicate the template they'd created. Jill had. What happened to me?

The funeral was on Thursday. I put on a black and grey checked coat-dress with black buttons and brushed out my hair. It hung in soft shiny curls, a good hair day. But it looked like happy hair, so I pulled it back and tied it with a black velvet ribbon.

Michael and I picked up my mother. She walked to the car with her back straight, her hair perfectly done and her blue suit pressed. She hugged me and we held it a little longer than usual. And then she got in the back seat and pulled her skirt down over her knees.

Only the gleaming black hearse was in the parking lot when we arrived and the funeral home was still quiet. There were two enormous floral arrangements on either side of the glossy casket and rows of chairs lined up like soldiers. The funeral director spoke to us in quiet, efficient tones. Jill and Mark came in, then Sophie, Pete, Danielle and Tiffany, then other friends and family came in a steady stream, offering hugs, hands, comforting gestures. Michael stayed by my side watching me carefully as if afraid I would break. His solicitousness made me a little edgy but I felt so fragile that I thought perhaps he could keep me together.

The smell from the flowers was cloying and I longed to go back outside and take a deep breath of fresh air that smelled of grass and sunlight. I hadn't run in more than a week and I longed to lace up my Nikes and do a ten-miler through the forest preserve. Or maybe a fifteen-miler. Or twenty. I wanted to run far away from this funeral home and the casket with my father inside and this new life that I'd have to live, without him.

Twenty

Michael and I started planning our wedding right after the funeral. I was grateful to have a focus, something to fill my extra time and occupy my mind. There was so much to do, so many details to decide, so many places to visit, so many dresses to try on. I welcomed the busy-ness of it all. I felt my father watching me. I knew he'd be happy, pleased that he wouldn't have to worry about me any more.

Jill and Sophie were both alarmed at the speed with which our plans progressed.

"Why don't you slow down a bit, hon," Sophie suggested. "You don't have to rush it. It's not as if you're pregnant or anything."

Jill said, "It's too soon. Dad just died. Maybe you should give yourself some time to deal with that. There's lots of time to plan a wedding."

"It's okay," I told them. "I understand what you're saying but I'm all right. Dad would want this, he'd be happy I was going forward with it. And Michael's been so wonderful, I know he's the right man for me, the one I should spend my life with. It wasn't clear to me before but it is now."

I had convinced myself completely, pushing my grief to a separate partition in my brain, and if they themselves weren't convinced they were sure that I was. I was fifty years old, after all, not a kid. So they both backed off and threw themselves into the spirit of planning, wanting to be supportive. Sometimes I think they should have tried harder to talk me out of it but when I look back on that time I know that no one could have talked me out of anything.

Patrick emailed after the funeral with his condolences.

> **I know it's not easy,** he wrote. **I lost my folks twenty years ago in a car accident. The hardest part was that they were here one day and just gone the next, just like that. Just ripped from my life without any warning.** My heart went out to him and I cried as I read. **You must feel something like that since your dad hadn't been sick or anything. I guess all we can do is be happy for the time we had with them and keep their memories in our hearts.**
> **My thoughts are with you, Libby.**
> **Love,**
> **Patrick**

His words calmed me, it was as if he'd put his arms around me. It was a comfort that he understood what I was feeling. *Love, Patrick* he had said.

Patrick,
Thank you for your kind email. It's horrible
that you lost both your parents at once, and
in such a shocking way. It's unimaginable. I
don't know how you would get through
something like that.
Losing my father is the hardest thing I've
ever been through. He's my hero and such a
large part of my heart and I miss him so
much. People keep telling me it will get easier
but right now I don't believe it. Now it is so
raw and difficult and impossible, and I can't
talk about him without crying. Wouldn't you
think at 50 I'd be able to control myself?
Libby

A reply came back almost immediately.

Lib,
It doesn't matter how old you are - this is
your father. Don't feel like you need to
control yourself or keep from crying. You
need to feel what you're feeling to work
through it.
I went to a grief counselor when my folks
died. I don't hardly tell anyone that, it seems
such a wussy thing for a guy to do, but it
really helped me. I tried for a while just to
deal with it myself but I have to tell you I just
wasn't doing it. I'm sure there's something
like that in Chicago. Maybe you could look
into it. Death is a tough deal. I think the first

**time someone close to you dies it's sort of
unreal and hard to get your mind around.
If you want to talk I'm here. Or you can call
me just to cry if you want. If you need to do
that, just do it.
Love,
Patrick**

Ironically Michael and I decided on the Palmer
House for our wedding. We looked at the Drake, the
Peninsula Hotel and the University Club but we both
liked the Empire Room at the Palmer House the best.
And it was available on my father's birthday seven
months from now, which was the day we'd chosen. We
would have a brief ceremony on the little balcony at the
side of the room with the hundred or so guests standing
and watching, and there would be high-top tables
scattered throughout the room for an elegant reception.

"We can create an aisle that would lead from the
double doors to the stage so you can make an entrance,"
Stacy the wedding coordinator said. Tears filled my eyes
when I envisioned walking down an aisle without my
father. "Well, we don't have to have an aisle," she said
as tears streamed down my face.

"It's okay, sweetheart," Michael said, pulling me
close. He explained about my father and Stacy magically
remembered an important errand which would only take
five or ten minutes, giving the weepy bride a chance to
collect herself.

"It's okay," Michael said again when she'd gone,
and handed me a handkerchief. "It's an emotional time, I
know. Try to focus on the details and not concentrate on

your dad not being there. He'll be there in spirit." I wiped my face and handed him his back handkerchief. "Would you want my dad to walk you down the aisle?"

No, I wanted to scream, *I want my own father to walk me down the aisle.*

But Michael was just trying to help so I said I'd think about it.

Twenty-One

When Bea Rosatti came back from her cruise she called to see how I was doing. She needed some alterations done but assured me it was nothing she couldn't live without. "Whenever you're ready, dear," she said. "You just let me know."

"Thank you. But I need to work," I told her, and said I could come by in the afternoon if that worked for her.

"If you're sure," she said. "I have the whole afternoon free and a luscious chicken salad in the fridge. Come for lunch."

She was right. The chicken salad was luscious. It had grapes and almonds in it and she served it on nests of crisp lettuce with sliced tomatoes fanned out on the side of the plate.

"This is delicious," I said. "I want this recipe."

Bea's laugh was a bright tinkling sound.

"Okay but you'll have to call Whole Foods and ask them because that's where I got it. I did slave over the lettuce beds, though." She wore a bright pink sweater with ruffles on the collar and sleeves, and matching pink dangling earrings. She looked like cotton candy.

"How is your mother doing," she asked.

"She's okay. As well as can be expected, I suppose. She's a strong lady. I stayed with her before the funeral. And a couple days after. But then she told me to go home." I swallowed. "I guess she didn't need me any more." That was when I started to cry. All I did was cry these days. "I'm sorry," I said, using my napkin to mop my face.

"Don't be sorry. Cry." Bea put a box of tissues in front of me and poured sherry into small etched glasses. "It's not that she doesn't need you any more, Libby, you know that. I'm sure she felt guilty that you were spending so much time with her. I'm sure she doesn't want to be a burden. And she probably feels she needs to be strong for you."

"But she doesn't," I said. "It helps me to be there for her."

"Just tell her that. Now it's especially important to talk to each other." I blew my nose. "Who's there for you, honey?" Bea asked.

"My mom. Jill. Michael."

"What's happening with Michael?"

"He's been wonderful. Very strong and supportive." Bea sipped her sherry, played with an earring. "We're going ahead with our wedding plans," I said. She raised an eyebrow. "We're getting married on my dad's birthday. In seven months."

"Well, that's lovely," she said.

"Yes, I'm happy. It took my dad's death to make me see how important Michael is to me." Bea handed me a tissue. I hadn't even noticed that tears were running down my face again. "I don't know what's wrong with me," I said and laughed. "I don't know why I'm crying. I'm happy."

"You're happy and you're sad."

I nodded. "I don't know what I feel any more. Sometimes I feel like I can't function, like I can't think." A sob burst from my throat. "Sometimes I feel like I'm falling apart."

"Of course you do, Libby. Of course." Bea moved her chair close to mine and put her arm around me. She smelled of apples and spearmint. "It's a difficult time. It's hard to know if your emotions are real or if they're from grief. You just need to give yourself time. Don't expect too much from yourself."

I dried my eyes, downed my sherry and smiled. "Thanks, Bea." I stacked our plates. "I'm good now." She patted my shoulder and cleared the table. "Let's see what work you've got for me," I said.

She'd bought some things when she was on the cruise; lime green Capri pants with a navy and lime green jacket, a red dress with abstract splashes of white, all needing alterations.

"So how was the trip?" I asked as I pinned the jacket.

"Fabulous," she said. "I have pictures if you're interested."

"I'd love to see them." When I'd finished marking and pinning her clothes we looked at a small stack of photos. They were large format photos, professional ones taken by the ship's photographer.

"He's everywhere," Bea said, "snapping pictures at every opportunity and then they're posted on a board the next day and everyone searches for their photos and exclaims how expensive they are. And then they all buy every one of them. Just like we did."

There was the *Welcome Aboard* photo and the *Captain's Dinner* photo and then the disembarking photo at each port, Dominick and Bea waving to the camera as they stood on the gangplank. I leisurely went through the stack asking occasionally for an explanation, oohing and aahing at a beautiful sunset or a long shot of the ship looking like a floating building. There was a photo of their dinner table, eight smiling faces, everyone dressed in elegant clothing, Bea in something short-sleeved and red spangled. She and Dominick smiled at the camera while small red-haired children stood on each side of them, heads leaning on their shoulders. Behind them stood four adults; one obviously the mother of the children, a red head with wide-set eyes. Bea was holding up her left hand, displaying a glinting ring.

"What's this?" I said.

"Oh that," Bea said. "That's the night Dominick proposed."

My jaw dropped. "Proposed? Oh my god," I put down the pictures and hugged Bea's small body. "I'm so happy for you. That's wonderful." I pulled back and looked at her radiant face. "I can't believe you kept quiet about this all this time."

"It didn't seem like the right time," she said.

"Oh it is. Truly. I'm so happy for you. Let me see that rock." I took her small hand. "How did I miss that?"

"You have other things on your mind," she said.

"It's beautiful." It was simple and elegant but quite large, and I thought about my own ring sitting in its box in the dresser drawer. I hadn't had it sized yet. Hadn't even taken it to the jeweler.

"Isn't this silly?" she said. "An engagement ring at seventy-six." But she was clearly delighted.

"It's not silly, It's lovely. Were you expecting this?" I asked.

"Not at all."

"Did he ask you in front of all these people?"

"Yes. Pretty sure of himself wasn't he?"

I laughed. "I'll say. Very gutsy." I was thinking Michael had pretty much done the same kind of thing and it didn't turn out so well for him. At least not at first.

"They all knew about it before I did," Bea said.

"You're kidding. Did you know these people before you went on the cruise?"

"No, they were just our table mates but it was the fourth night of the cruise and we'd all become fond of one another by that time. So he secretly told them what he was planning and swore them to secrecy. They were nervous as cats, especially the little twins, but there was a chocolate tasting on the Lido deck in the afternoon and I thought they were all just on a sugar rush."

"How did he ask you?"

"The waiter served me the ring on a silver tray with a lid. We all had trays with lids and the waiters stood behind us and lifted the lids simultaneously and everyone but me had a lovely piece of fish. I had a small velvet box on my tray."

"How romantic."

"Yes it was. And then Dominick took my hand and asked me to marry him and opened the little box to show me this beautiful ring and I cried and said yes and then the entire dining room burst into applause." Her eyes flashed at the memory and she laughed.

"Oh my."

"And then some musicians came over and played Unforgettable," she said. "It was all terribly romantic."

"So how do you feel?" I didn't need to ask. Her face was like a display window into her delight.

"Like a schoolgirl," she said, and I felt a little twinge of jealousy.

"I'm so happy for you. It's wonderful."

"Thank you dear. I knew you'd be happy."

I remembered the day I had come to her house when she and Dominick had been quiet and cautious with each other. It was the day Dominick had first brought up the idea of living together.

"It wasn't so long ago that you were unsure about moving in together," I said, "and now you're getting married. What changed your mind?"

"I think when Dominick first brought up the idea it just caught me off-guard. But after we talked about it and I really considered it, it started to feel right, comfortable. And then I wondered why I *hadn't* considered it before.

"It's nice to think about having someone to spend my old age with," she said. "Not that I plan on being old."

"And you never will be," I said. "Well, it's wonderful, inspiring." We looked through the rest of the pictures. "My wedding gift to you will be your wedding dress," I said. "You tell me exactly what you want; a dress, a suit, whatever and I'll design it and make it for you."

"Oh Libby, that's fabulous," she said, clapping her hands. "It'll be my honor to wear an original Libby for my wedding." *Original Libby*. I liked the way that sounded.

"Are you going to make your own dress for your wedding?" she asked.

"No," I said. "I thought I'd just buy one. Michael's going to help me pick it out."

"Michael!" she said. "Michael shouldn't help. Take your mom or your sister but not Michael. That's bad luck."

As I drove home I smiled at Bea's superstition. It was silly, really. It wasn't as if I were twenty years old, getting married for the first time, looking for a traditional white Cinderella-style wedding gown. What did it matter who helped me pick out the dress?

But then I thought there was no point in pressing my luck and decided I'd make an outing of it and ask my mom and Jill and Sophie instead.

Twenty-Two

Libby,
I've been thinking about you and hope
you're doing well. The weather's warm here
and the sunset was beautiful last night. I had
two kayak tours yesterday, one with 4 macho
guys who were body-building, extreme sports
types, so I'm relaxing today. My 50 year old
body was pushed to the limit.
I found some information on grief counseling
in the Chicago area and thought I'd pass it
along. I hope you're not offended, I don't
even know if this is right for you, I was just
doing a little research and thought I'd let you
know. Just in case.
He gave me phone numbers and web addresses
for two options and signed his email,
Love,
Patrick

Even though I wasn't sure I was ready for something like that I felt the way I would if he'd put a home-knitted afghan around my shoulders. I looked at one of the sites which said the group was for people who have suffered the loss of someone significant; a parent, sibling, spouse, child. It said that the participants share their experience and learn about the grieving process. "Although grief is a normal human experience," it said, "everyone experiences grief in his or her own way. Our group helps you cope with your loss and understand the feelings that come with change. We can help you regain your balance as you learn to accept your life in a new way."

Balance would be good, I thought, and sat staring at the faces on the website of the counselors; Rebecca, a thin, older woman with curly blonde hair, and Henry, a gray-haired man with a kindly priest-like face and rimless glasses.

Patrick,
Thanks for the info. I'm not offended at all.
It was sweet of you. I'm trying to get back on
an even keel. It's not been easy but of course
it's all still fresh and tender. I read one of the
websites and am giving it some thought.
Michael and I are going ahead with our
wedding plans. We're getting married on my
father's birthday in seven months. I know
that my father would be very happy about
this.
Libby

"Where are we going?" I asked Michael as we drove through the quiet streets of my neighborhood.

He'd called in the afternoon to see if I was home and available. For a little field trip, he'd said. "I have something I want to show you."

"What is it?"

"A surprise," he'd said. "I'll be over in half an hour."

"You'll see in a second," he said now. His voice held excitement like a little kid's. He turned down Marshall Street and then made a quick left on Cherry. There my favorite house sat proudly with its white picket fence and wrap-around porch. He stopped in front. I looked at him. His eyes were shining and a smile was ready to burst right off of his face.

"Your favorite house," he said. "For sale."

"Yes, I see," I said.

"I made an offer on it."

I stared at him. "What do you mean you made an offer on it?"

"Just what I said, I made an offer on it."

"You're kidding."

"Nope."

"Wow." What else was there to say?

"My offer was accepted," he said.

Now I was dumbfounded. "You *bought* it?"

"Yes. Can you believe it?" The car could barely contain his excitement. "You always said whoever lived in that house would just have to be happy."

"But Michael, I have a house."

"I know but that's *your* house not *ours*. This old couple lives here. They've been here since they got married. They're so cute. When I told them about how you always loved this house and that I was going to surprise you they were so excited."

His eyes shone. He was so eager and proud of this surprise.

"How did this happen?" I asked.

"It came on the market and I was looking at the new listings and when I saw it I called the listing agent and we went right over and made them an offer and they accepted it. It all happened so fast."

I sighed. "What if I don't want to live here, Michael? What if I don't want to sell my house?"

"Why wouldn't you want to live here? You love this house."

"What if it's not what I think it is?"

Michael laughed. "Let me assure you it's not. It definitely needs work. But we'll make it whatever you want it to be. I got it for a good price. We can live in your house while we remodel this one. And then we can sell your house." *Sell my house*? All these plans, he had it all figured out. It was making my head swim.

He moved close to me and put his arm around me. "Let's go see it."

I stared out the window not trusting myself to talk, agitation bubbling up inside like an oil gusher. I was torn between wanting to run screaming from the car and the overwhelming desire to finally see my dream house.

He reached for the door handle. "Come on," he said.

"We can't just go inside," I said.

"It's okay, hon, they won't mind," he said. "I told them we might be by this afternoon. They're expecting us. They're anxious to meet you."

Fear, excitement, distress, gratitude all swirled through my head like dust devils. But I got out of the car and Michael and I walked up to the door. White rockers sat on the porch and for a moment I got a pleasant little picture of us having a glass of wine out here on warm evenings.

The Stroms looked like they were blood related; they were both ample people with big open faces and wide smiles showing yellowed teeth. Their bulldog Frank hung just behind their feet looking up at Michael and me with the same expression. He could've been their offspring.

"Oh Libby, so nice to meet you," Mrs. Strom trilled, grasping my hand. "Michael told us so much about you."

"It's nice to meet you too," I said.

We stood in the entryway. Ahead of us was a wide stairway to the second floor, the living room to the right and the dining room to the left. On the floor where we stood was olive-green shag carpeting that had obviously been here a while, maybe ever since it was trendy, in the 60s. There was a bentwood coat rack against one wall and a large blue and white urn on the other filled with plastic zinnias in a rainbow of colors, thickly covered with dust. The walls were covered in faded green and gold wallpaper.

"Come in. Would you like something to drink?" Mr. Strom asked, leading the way into the kitchen. "Mother, you forgot to do the breakfast dishes," he observed. He patted his wife's shoulder and clucked his tongue. If the dishes were all from this morning they must have had the front line of the Chicago Bears as guests. There were dirty pans on the stove and the sink was piled high with dishes and glassware. I wondered if there were any clean glasses in the cupboards. No matter. After seeing this, the probability that I would accept a food item from this house was as likely as finding a Jacuzzi in their marble bathroom.

"No thank you," Michael and I said in unison.

"Well, so this is the kitchen," Mrs. Strom said. "There's lots of cupboard space." With her cane she walked slowly around the room opening cupboards. Her thick bow-legs looked painful to walk on. Mr. Strom helped her along, sweetly gripping her arm.

"We ate our meals right here in this very room for sixty years," she said indicating a chrome table with a Formica top. The chairs had thick brown vinyl seats with duct tape patches.

It was far from the image I'd had of this house. It didn't fit into my *Father Knows Best* fantasy although it probably had some of the same furnishings. *Vintage* was how Michael, as a realtor, would describe it. *Tear-down* was how I'd describe it.

"Great space, isn't it?" Michael said. "This is such a great kitchen." I forced a cough to cover up the laughter bubbling up in my throat. The Stroms beamed at him as I pictured a team of workmen in hardhats with sledgehammers going to work on the walls and appliances. By now I had seen as much as I wanted to see. If I got out now I could preserve a little part of my dream.

No such luck.

"Let's go this way. The dining room's right through there," Mr. Strom said, taking his wife's arm and laboriously leading the way.

By the time we had worked our way upstairs and were peering into the only bathroom I was nearly delirious with revulsion. Brown one-inch square tiles covered the floor and climbed halfway up the walls. Worn, dark paneling covered the top half. There was a tiny little sink set into a vanity which was yellowed-white with brown trim and had a counter made of fake marble. Also in dark brown. Two people could occupy this bathroom at the same time but only if they were conjoined twins.

"Well," I said brightly, "thank you so much for your hospitality but we really must be going."

"Oh, it's our pleasure dear," Mrs. Strom said. "We're so happy you all bought it. Can you stay for tea and cookies? I made oatmeal raisin cookies yesterday. Papa's favorite."

Mr. Strom nodded happily. "They're the best," he said. "Mother missed her calling. I always told her she should have packaged them and sold them. We could have been billionaires."

"That's very kind of you," I said. "But we have an appointment we need to get to."

Michael smiled at them and grasped their hands warmly. "Thanks so much," he said. "This is a great house. I'm very excited."

At the door when we were finally close to our escape, Mrs. Strom said to me, "I know you'll be very happy here. It's a happy house."

Michael smiled as he drove back to my house, my clean, neat, updated house with its hardwood floors and granite countertops. "It has great bones, doesn't it?" he asked.

"Bones are all it has," I said. "It would cost a fortune to make that place livable, Michael."

"Well, yeah, it'll cost some bucks. But don't you think it's like fate that it went up for sale now? It's like it's meant to be, you know?"

"Well, you know I'm not a believer in stuff like that but I admit the timing is impressive." He laughed.

"We need to talk about this, though. You're doing it again, making decisions for us, decisions we need to make together. I've had enough surprises to last me a lifetime." He flinched and looked wounded, making me regret my words. "It's a wonderful surprise, Michael, but it's a big thing. We've got to both be invested in this. Let's just talk about it before we do anything rash."

"I have a contract on it."

Jesus, what was with the strong-arm tactics?

"I understand that. But you acted impulsively and it may not have been the best decision." He sighed. "No more surprises, Michael. Promise me. You need to save the surprises for the small stuff not for something this big."

He sighed again.

"Promise me, Michael."

"All right, I promise," he said, and we drove the rest of the way in silence.

Twenty-Three

I wondered if I'd continue to hear from Patrick after telling him about my wedding plans but he seemed unfazed. A smile always came to my lips when I saw his screen name in my in-box.

Libby,
I'm happy for you and Michael. He's a lucky
guy. How are the wedding plans coming
along? Is it going to be a big blow-out affair?
How are you doing? How are you feeling?
Have you looked into grief counseling? I
don't mean to be pushy, just curious. One of
the things it gave me was a place where I
could talk about my parents and no one
would tell me I should think about something
else. That helped me a lot. Also, another
thing I thought was a really good idea was
writing a letter to the person who died. They
said it helps you understand your feelings

and is a way to say things you can't say in
person any more. I'm not much of a
writer but it was good for me.
Love,
Patrick

Patrick, I wrote back, Always nice to hear
from you. I'm doing okay. Good days, bad
days...you know. I like the idea of a letter to
my father. I'll try that sometime.
I do really appreciate your suggestions and I
don't feel like you're nagging or anything.
Some people seem to think I should move on,
get over it. It's hard. Sometimes I feel like I
have to put up a front so other people won't
be upset. That's fucked up, don't you think?
I hope I never did that to anyone who was
mourning a loved one.
Michael and I are having a small wedding,
about 80 people. We're getting married on
my father's birthday. It just seemed right to
me. A judge will marry us in a very brief
ceremony and then a cocktail party
following. Heavy hors d'oeuvres and
cocktails. My mom will walk with me down
the aisle.
Michael bought a house yesterday and didn't
tell me. It's a house I've always loved in the
neighborhood and it came up for sale and he
put in an offer to surprise me (Michael's a
realtor, did I tell you that?) and his offer was
accepted. My head's spinning. The house is a
mess. Needs billions of dollars in renovations.
I can't even think about it.

Jill and I are going to a bereavement group, one of the ones you told me about. I'm nervous. We both are. Nervous, anxious, scared. But there's also a little relief in it.

Write me soon.
Libby

The room was decorated in soothing shades of forest green and burgundy. One wall was lined with bookshelves and there were plants and snow globes among the books. Comfy chairs were placed in a semi-circle in front of a fireplace and there were two women already seated, sipping coffee from thick mugs, talking quietly when Jill and I walked in. They looked up and smiled. It was all very warm and welcoming, homey. I burst into tears.

A man came toward us, hand outstretched, tissue box in hand. "Welcome," he said. "I'm Henry." I recognized him from his picture on the website. He was taller than I expected, heavier, a little older. His silver hair was cut very short and he wore a plaid shirt under a cardigan sweater. "Don't worry," he said as I wiped my face. "It happens to a lot of people."

We introduced ourselves and then he introduced us to the two women, Carlyn and Lisa, and offered us coffee. People drifted in while we stirred cream and sugar into our mugs. My stomach churned. I didn't know what to expect. I guess I thought everyone would be sobbing into shredded tissues but these people all seemed calm to me, peaceful.

"You okay?" Jill asked.

"I don't know. You?"

"I don't know," she said. "I'm not sure I want to talk about how I feel with a bunch of strangers."

"Me either. But I'm sure we don't have to say anything if we don't want to," I told her. I wasn't really sure of anything.

The session began with everyone introducing themselves, just their names and why they were here. There were eight of us; two men and six women, four who'd lost parents, two who'd lost spouses, one who'd lost an aunt, and Carlyn who'd lost a three year old child. She told her story dry-eyed but sorrow etched her face and I wiped my own tears as she spoke.

When we were finished Henry said, "There is no greater stress to the human system than death. Everyone grieves differently and no one's loss is greater or lesser than anyone else's." I was sure the death of a three year old trumped all of us. "Sometimes when we suffer a great loss we lose our perspective, our sense of self-worth. We question our reasons to go on. But as trite as it sounds, life does goes on, and healing comes when you reach out and embrace your own life.

"Mourning is hard work. It's exhausting. It can feel as if every little action requires super-human strength. But we'll do it a step at a time. Don't move too fast at first. Don't expect too much of yourself. And don't let anyone else tell you how to grieve."

My spine softened, my shoulders relaxed a bit. I leaned back into my chair.

"For the time we're together we're going to be kind to each other and patient. We're going to help each other. This is a safe place where you can talk and cry and gain strength. It's a place where you'll learn that it's okay to laugh again. In here we'll learn to live the rest of our lives in a new way."

Jill and I were both tired as we drove home. "That wasn't bad," she said.

"No. It was good. Even though I cried the whole time."

"You're a cryer. Always have been."

"Yeah. You'd think I'd outgrow that."

"There's still time," Jill said. "You're only fifty."

The night was cool and clear. I opened my window a crack to let fresh air blow on my puffy face. I liked the feel of my hair blowing off my face. "I think it helps to be with people who know what you're feeling," I said.

"I wish we could have talked Mom into coming with us."

"It's not her thing. She comes from the don't-talk-about-it-and-it-will-go-away school of thought. They both did. Dad always told me to turn the other cheek, especially about men. He thought you should just shut up and accept things. He never saw the good in talking things through."

"I know. I think it's the time they grew up in. People weren't so open in their generation."

The streets were peaceful as we got closer to my house. "Remember that house on Cherry Street?" I said. "The one with the white picket fence?"

"The *Father Knows Best* house? I love that house."

"Michael bought it for us."

"You're kidding," Jill said. "That's so cool. I didn't even know you were looking for a house."

"I didn't either. He did it on his own. Didn't even mention it to me until it was a done deal."

Jill turned to look at me. Then back at the road. "Libby, what the fuck?"

"I know. I know."

"You can't do that when you're a couple. Part of being married is working together, having common goals." She was more indignant than I would have thought, and it made me feel defensive of Michael.

"Calm down, Jill. It's not that bad. He knew I loved that house. He wanted to surprise me."

"You don't surprise someone with a *house*, for Christ's sake. It's not like a new blender. Jesus. What if you didn't like it?"

"But I did like it. He knew that."

I couldn't bring myself to describe it or tell her how much it was going to cost to remodel. I wished I hadn't said anything. Her reaction made me feel worse than I already did.

"Still…" she said.

We rode in silence for a while which was fine with me since I didn't want to hear what she was thinking. She avoided Cherry Street, driving down Maple instead, three blocks out of our way. When she pulled in front of my house I said, "Thanks for driving," and started to open my door. Jill put the car in *Park* and turned to me. "Don't go yet, Lib, I want to say something."

No, don't, I thought, but shut the door and looked at her. Her face was serious in the half-light from the streetlamp. She looked like she did when she was four and told me our dog had died while I was at school. She had the same frown, the same penetrating look in her eyes.

"In the spirit of being open," she said, "and not being an ignore-it-and-it'll-go-away kind of person…"

She smiled. I didn't. "You know what Henry said about not making big life changes after a major loss? Remember? He said we shouldn't make any important decisions until our lives feel more on track?"

"I remember."

"You're doing it in spades, Libby. Getting married, moving, selling your house…it's a lot. You're like the poster child for what he said not to do."

"Michael and I were already engaged."

"But you weren't sure you were going to marry him. Remember that? You were questioning the whole thing. Then Dad dies and all of a sudden you're sure. It's not a decision that was already made." She took my hand. "I'm not saying don't do it, Lib, you know that. I'm just saying wait a little while. What's the hurry?"

I took my hand away. "I don't see the point in waiting."

"But what's the harm?"

"We already have the Empire Room booked, we bought the invitations, we hired a photographer."

"I know. But still…"

"And I think Dad would be happy about it," I said. My trump card.

Jill studied her perfectly manicured nails, bit at an imaginary hangnail. "I don't think so," she said.

My eyes welled with tears. As if I hadn't cried enough today. "Jesus, what's wrong with you? What are you saying? One minute you tell me to marry Michael and the next you tell me not to. *Make up your mind!*" I said. I opened my door. "I'm going in now," I said and got out of the car.

"Lib," she called after me. "Don't go."

I stood for a moment, shaking. I bent and looked in at her. "Thanks for your concern, really, but I know what I'm doing."

"I'm just worried about you," she said. Her eyes were dark with sadness. My little sister.

I got back in the car, dug into my purse for a tissue and blew my nose. "I have a stomach ache all the time, Jill. I can't sleep. I miss him so much. I feel like a part of me is missing."

"I do too," she said.

I'd been so wrapped up in my own loss and Jill was so stoical that I'd just ignored the fact that he was her father too. "I know, hon," I said rubbing her shoulder. "I know that. I know you're in pain." I hugged her. "But Dad didn't worry about you the way he worried about me. You're married. That was the difference. He wanted that for me. Michael has a lot of the same qualities as Dad. He's a good, kind man who'll take care of me. And I feel like he can fill that hole for me. How can that be bad?"

"No one can fill that hole. You have to learn how to live with it. Keep things simple for a while and then figure out where Michael fits."

I sighed. I yawned. "I can't talk any more, Jill. I'm exhausted. I'm done. I'm going in now." I wanted to climb in bed, pull the covers over my head and sleep until I didn't feel like this any more.

"I'll call you tomorrow," Jill said. "I'll support you no matter what you decide to do, promise. I love you, Lib."

"I love you too," I said.

I couldn't get out of the car fast enough.

Twenty-Four

Dear Daddy, I wrote that night when I woke at 2:30 a.m. and couldn't go back to sleep. *I miss you so much. I've never believed in an afterlife but I can't bear the thought that you are just gone. I need to feel that you're still with me. Sometimes I feel you watching me. But I want something tangible. I want a sign.*

Tonight I had a dream that I was transporting your body somewhere, I don't know where. I knew you were dead but you were sitting in a chair, a wheelchair-type thing with a high back. You reached up and rubbed your nose. I stared at you for a minute and then I said, "Daddy, are you okay?" and you said, "My nose itches," and I said, "But you're dead," and you said, "I know."

We talked for a while, I don't know what about, and then I said, "I wish you weren't dead," and you said, "I know you do, honey, but it's really better this way. I'm okay." I said, "I love you so much, Dad," and you said, "I love you too, honey." And then I woke up. I

cried a little but really, I feet sort of peaceful cuz you'd
said you were okay.
     Was that my sign?
     I love you,
     Libby

When I finished I sat quietly at my desk waiting
for my answer. The house was quiet. Rufus was still
asleep on my bed. The furnace purred, the refrigerator
hummed, I heard a siren far off in the distance. If any of
that was a sign it was too subtle for me.

I didn't feel sleepy enough to go back to bed so I
went to my computer and was glad to see an email from
Patrick. It made my heart pound a little and made me
feel less alone.

Libby,
How'd the session go? I hope it was
worthwhile. And not too tough. I remember
the first one I went to I didn't think I'd go
back – all those people sitting around
emoting was a little much for me – but the
next day I felt calmer. So I did go back. And
I'm glad I did. It was a good thing for me.
I have to tell you this, Lib, and that is that
I'm worried about you. One thing I
remember from the group I went to – the
woman who led it said we shouldn't make
any big changes in our lives for at least a
year. That keeps going through my mind.
I've hesitated saying anything because I
don't want to piss you off by butting in
where I don't belong. I've been going back
and forth, having conversations with you in

**my mind, and I decided that since I'm your
friend I'm just going to tell you what I'm
thinking and you can ignore it if you want.
Getting married is a big change. I know you
and Michael have been together for years but
still…you live separately and even though
you're a couple you're still single. So I'm just
bringing it up as something for you to think
about. I'm not recommending anything one
way or the other, I just want you to think
about the decisions you're making now and
be sure you're not rushing into something
out of your grief and a need to put things in
some kind of order. I think the kicker for me
was the house thing. Wow. That sort of
freaked me out.
So there it is. I hope you're not upset by my
words. I promise I won't mention it again.
Love,
Patrick**

What was with everybody? Why did it seem so
much like the right decision to me while people all
around me saw it so differently? I wasn't angry with
Patrick for saying what he did. But I didn't answer him
either. I did add a P.S. to the letter to my father though.

*Here's what I need to know, Dad: You're happy
I'm marrying Michael, right?*

I went to the kitchen and poured myself a glass of
Pinot Grigio. I looked into it and studied it for several
moments. For what? My dad's face reflecting back at
me? Maybe a big *Yes* or *No* written in clouds on the
surface? But it was just wine. So I took it to the living
room, curled up on the couch with the afghan, and

contemplated the fact that I was past middle age, practically a senior citizen, and still I felt like a lost child.

Twenty-Five

Libby,
I haven't heard from you in a while and just want to
make sure everything's okay. I hope you're not upset
about what I said about not making big changes right
now. I didn't mean to imply you shouldn't get
married. I'm not involved in your life - I don't see
you regularly so what I said was meant to be taken
with a grain of salt, okay? If you think now is a good
time to be married, if you're happy about the house,
then I am too. You're a big girl and I'm sure you
know what you're doing.
How is everything going? How are you feeling these
days?
It's so great being in touch with Pete and Sophie. I
talked to Pete on the phone the other day for about
an hour. They're thinking of making a trip down
here, did they tell you? Sometime after their
daughter's wedding. Maybe you could come with
them. With Michael, of course. I have a big house,
room for everyone, not far from the beach.
E me.
Love,
Patrick

The idea of all of us visiting Patrick seemed ludicrous. I could just imagine the scene, Michael and Patrick meeting in the hallway, towels wrapped around their waists, toothbrushes in hand. I laughed out loud. I could see all of us in pajamas and fuzzy slippers making breakfast. It had been a long time since I'd traveled with Sophie and Pete and it actually sounded like fun. An opinion Michael was sure to dispute.

I hadn't answered Patrick's last email. I had been irked. I don't like being told I'm making a mistake when I'm so sure of what I'm doing. Never did. My first reaction was always defensive. But Patrick had only expressed an opinion. And I supposed it was my best interests he had at heart. Or was there a hidden agenda in his words? My ego wanted both. And then, of course, there was that *Love, Patrick* at the end of every email that gave me a little golden glow every time he wrote it even though I never wrote it back.

> **Patrick,**
> **I'm not upset with you. I do appreciate your concern and am giving consideration to your words. I realize you're not trying to tell me what to do, just tell me what you think and that's fine.**
> **I'm doing okay. Life goes on, as they say, but the pain doesn't go away. I guess you just learn to live with it although that's not happening so quickly either. The bereavement group is a big help to me and to my sister so thank you for telling me about that. There's something comforting about being with people who know what you're going through.**
> **I wrote a letter to my dad as you suggested. In fact I've written a couple. I like doing it - it makes me feel that he's close. Unfortunately he's not answering my questions but I'm thinking he's putting the answers out there in the universe somewhere for me to find**

**them. He always encouraged my independence so
why start now making it easy for me?
I'm glad you and Pete have rekindled your
friendship. It still sort of amazes me to be in touch
with you after all these years. I can't imagine Michael
and me coming to Florida with Sophie and Pete. It's
such a funny idea. Not that it wouldn't be fun. But
thanks for the invitation. I hope S and P make it, tho.
Libby**

"I thought I was going to help you pick out your dress," Michael said in a whiney tone when I told him I was going shopping with the triumvirate: my mother, Jill and Sophie. I regarded him as he put on one black sock then a shoe, and reached for his other sock.

"Why don't you put both socks on first, then your shoes?" I asked.

He looked at his bare foot, then at me. "I don't know. I've always done it this way."

"I know. I've always thought it was weird. What if there was a fire? You'd be running out in the street with one bare foot."

He laughed and shook his head. "Talk about weird," he said, and put on his other sock and shoe. "So how come I'm not shopping with you?"

"It's bad luck for the groom to see the dress before the wedding."

"It's bad luck for the bride to wear a dress the groom doesn't like."

"You think I'll pick out something you wouldn't like? You always like what I wear." Michael watched his reflection as he tied a red striped tie over his blue shirt. "Don't you?" I asked.

"Sure," he said. "I just thought it would be a nice thing to do together."

I put on a white V-neck sweater and black pants. Michael was spending more and more time at my house. He seemed to be moving in by centimeters, a pair of socks in the laundry basket, jockey shorts in a drawer, more pants hanging in the closet. We hadn't talked about it, it was just happening. It's hard now to imagine that I just went along with it but at the time I didn't have the energy for the confrontation a discussion would surely cause. Besides, he was my fiancé. What was there to discuss?

"Maybe you could take a picture with your cell phone and send it to me before you buy anything," he said.

"Maybe you could just wait and be surprised," I said. He pulled the tie apart, apparently not satisfied, and started re-knotting it.

"You never used to be so controlling," I told him.

He met my eyes in the mirror. "Controlling?"

"Yes, controlling."

"How so?"

"*How so?* Let me count the ways."

"Hmmm. Okay then, don't email a picture and I'll be surprised," he said and finished knotting his tie.

I stood on a pedestal in front of a tri-fold mirror, swathed in fluffy silk organza while the bridal consultant and my mother ooh'd and aah'd. Sophie and Jill both wore expressions that said, "*Oh, please.*"

"You look like you're twenty years old in that," my mom said.

"Yeah, if you don't look at my fifty year old face."

"You're *fifty*?" Cara, the bridal consultant, said with such incredulity that I wanted to hug her and buy the damn dress. "I thought you were in your thirties," she said. Bless her little lying heart.

If Jill was still concerned about me marrying Michael now and making so many life changes, she hid it well and got into the spirit of the day, moving from rack to rack, offering up various options. Ultimately we'd all picked out four dresses, the big puffy thing being my mother's, of course, and I was the human mannequin.

"It's a bit much, Mom. I know you love this style but this wedding is going to be more like a fancy cocktail party with a marriage ceremony thrown in. Did you pick out anything less frou-frou?"

"No," she said. "But try them on anyway." So I did, while Jill yawned and Sophie filed her nails.

Sophie's and Jill's choices ran more toward mother-of-the-bride styles; elegant suits and conservative tea length dresses. Mine were less conventional; a slinky black beaded dress with a silver shawl, a knee-length burgundy silk skirt and sequined top, a red evening gown with a fringed jacket.

By the time I got to the last dress we were all worn out and I was no closer to buying a dress than I'd been when we walked in. I could only imagine what we looked like to Cara; three middle-aged women and a senior citizen, slouched in our chairs, bags under our eyes, hair disheveled. She wore a little half smile as she re-hung the last of the dresses. "I'm going to go get you each a glass of wine," she said, and we all perked up. "And then I'm going to bring one last dress for you to try on." I groaned. "I know," she said, "but I think I know what you're looking for." How could she know? She was twelve. But what was one more dress? Besides I really wanted that wine.

We sat in exhausted silence sipping our wine and nibbling on the cookies she'd brought, until Sophie said, "Pete talked to Patrick the other day and invited him to come to Danielle's wedding."

I stopped chewing. Patrick, here? At Danielle's wedding? Patrick and Michael in the same room? "Why'd he do that?"

"He's just so happy to be in touch with him. It's like he has a new best friend. He wants to get together and I think it just came out." She shrugged. "I think he might come."

I swallowed. "Well, well," Jill said. "Things keep getting curiouser and curiouser."

"Who's Patrick?" my mother asked.

"Libby's high school boyfriend," Jill said. "Remember the guy with the long hair and the black leather that you and Daddy hated?"

"Oh I'm sure that's not true," my mother said. "We never hated anyone Libby dated."

Jill and Sophie and I laughed. "Well, you weren't crazy about his long hair," I said. "Do you remember him?"

"Oh honey, I barely remember you. How could I remember someone you dated in high school?"

"Remember the Bradshaws?" Jill asked. I gave her a look but she kept going. "Remember when Libby went to a New Year's Eve party at their house?"

"No, dear, I don't remember. And I'm not going to tax my brain. But what's the difference? It's all ancient history." She looked at me. "Have you kept in touch with him?"

"Just recently we got in touch through a website where people find their high school friends."

"SearchForSchoolmates.com?" my mother asked.

I almost dropped my wine glass. "How do you know about that?"

"Do you think I sit around and knit all day?" she said. "I'm the computer queen of my book club. I've taught everyone how to use a computer. I've been on that website a number of times. Although as you can imagine there aren't many of my classmates left."

My mother on SearchForSchoolmates.com. Amazing. What if she was emailing old boyfriends?

"Who'd you find?" Sophie asked, clearly delighted with the idea.

"I found a girl I used to run around with, Sarah Posen."

"Does she live here in Chicago?"

"No, in Michigan. Not too far, though. We're going to try to get together soon. I'd love to see her. Haven't laid eyes on her in about sixty years."

"Technology is amazing, isn't it?" Jill said.

"It is," I said. "How would we have gotten in touch with these people years ago? It would have taken so much effort that no one would have ever bothered. Now it's as simple as having a computer and an Internet connection, and you can get reacquainted with someone you haven't seen in sixty years."

"Or thirty," Sophie said.

Cara came back with an elegant ankle-length crocheted tank dress and matching jacket in a shimmery bronze color. It was shot through with metallic shine and there were tiers of scalloped lace at the hem. We all nodded when we saw it, our heads bobbing, smiles on our faces. And when I tried it on there was consensus. It was perfect. I had a wedding dress.

Twenty-Six

The next two weeks were a blur of activity, which was good. It kept me from dwelling on the fact that my father was dead, that I would never hear his laugh again or touch his hand. There were long stretches of time when I just spaced out, couldn't think what I was doing or where I was going and then I'd come to because I had to pay attention to Michael's details and all his various plans.

He decided to sell his condo and in two days had a contract with a co-worker who'd often expressed interest in it. Why was everything happening so fast? First the *Father Knows Best* house and now this. It was as if Michael had a golden touch.

He wasn't closing for eight weeks but he'd already started packing and bringing things to my house box by box; kitchen things, picture albums, books - things I had no room or use for, and the boxes went straight to the basement for storage, stacked up like little condos.

He called an architect and we had meetings to discuss renovations on the new house, even though it wouldn't be ours for two months. Everything was moving at warp speed but I went along, just floating on the current of activity.

I worked with Bea Rosatti on her wedding outfit, which was to be a fitted, knee-length dress with long sleeves and V-neck, and a jacket with a ruffle down the front and on the sleeves. I'd sketched out several options for her and she'd surprised me by picking the most conservative one. But when we went shopping for fabric my elegant, dignified design morphed into something very Bea-like when she picked a watermelon-colored silky, glitzy, sparkly fabric that turned out to be a challenge to work with.

And during those weeks, the two weeks before Danielle's wedding, Patrick and I exchanged emails about his upcoming trip to Chicago. He was excited to see Sophie and Pete again and to meet their daughters. He was happy he would be seeing me again so soon, which warmed my heart. And he was looking forward to meeting Michael. At least that's what he said.

When I told Michael about it he was less than thrilled.

"That's ridiculous," he said. "Why would Pete invite him? He hasn't seen him since high school."

"I suppose that's why," I said. "He's happy to be in touch with him again."

"If he wanted to be in touch with him so badly why didn't he make an effort all these years?"

Michael's tone was exasperating. I had no desire to have a conversation about it so I left the room, went to my workroom and picked up Bea's dress, cut out the facings, pinned them to the armholes. Michael followed me. I pretended not to notice.

"He's just coming because he wants to see you," he said. I almost smiled at the thought. When I didn't reply Michael said, "How do you feel about it?"

I looked up from my work, peering at him over my reading glasses. "I feel fine about it. It'll be nice to see him again."

"Again?"

Oops. I'd forgotten that Michael didn't know Patrick had come to Chicago to have lunch with me. It seemed so long ago now.

So I told him.

"You're kidding," he said when I'd finished.

"I'm not," I said, and continued pinning.

"Wait, let me get this straight. He flew 1500 miles to have lunch with you."

"That's right."

I could feel Michael's eyes on me but I just continued pinning, one after the other.

"What's with this guy? Does he have his own plane?"

"He's a little impulsive," I said.

"A *little*?"

I stabbed my finger with a pin and a small red bubble rose up. "Ouch. Goddamn it." I sucked on it and squelched the urge to tell Michael to shut up and get out. So what if Patrick was impulsive? What the hell did it matter? I put down the fabric, took off my glasses and looked at him, finger in my mouth.

"Let it go, Michael." I said it as quietly as I could.

"I can't," he said. "I hate this guy and I don't want him here."

I laughed out loud. Not because I was amused but because Michael sounded like a ten year old instead of a man nearing sixty. I imagined him throwing himself to the floor, kicking his legs.

"You don't even know him. And anyway it's not up to you. Pete invited him and he's coming. He's just a guy, Michael."

Michael narrowed his eyes.

"You're jealous," I said.

"I'm not jealous. I just think the whole thing's stupid."

"Well, fine, think it's stupid. It is what it is and you're going to have to deal with it and it would be nice if you'd act like a grown-up about it." He stared, eyes blazing. I could see all the retorts bubbling up behind his lips which were locked in a tight line, and braced myself.

He turned and walked away.

"I'm marrying *you*, Michael," I said to his rigid back as he walked up the stairs. "I bought a dress, remember?" And reserved the room and called the caterer and had invitations engraved.

Twenty-Seven

The day of Danielle's wedding was bright and clear, and the church was dazzling white in the sunshine. It was like a movie-set church with stained-glass windows and an ornate spire reaching to the cloudless sky. Michael smiled at me and took my hand as we walked up the steps.

"Psssst," I heard when we were in the vestibule. There was a door off to the side and Tiffany's delicate face peeked out. She glowed, and I could see lots of lively purple behind her as the girls moved around the room. She grinned and waved, and I heard giggling as she shut the door. Michael and I smiled at each other and headed into the church.

"Bride's side or groom's?" the usher asked. He was young and handsome, hair gleaming blackly, styled with gel. He wore a black tuxedo with a purple cummerbund and bow tie.

"Bride's," I said and he offered his arm and walked me down the aisle with Michael following. The organist played something soft and sleepy as the guests took their seats. I looked around at the expectant faces, happy and excited, and scanned the pews for Patrick but he wasn't there and I felt disappointed thinking he wasn't coming after all.

The music stopped for several seconds and the murmuring of voices ceased. When it began again the congregation collectively turned toward the back of the church. First came Sophie's parents who looked vibrant and healthy, then Pete's mom, looking frail but bright with happiness. The groom's mother and father came next and then Sophie, looking radiant and elegant in a champagne-colored suit with a peplum waist and ankle length skirt.

The poofy purple confections came next, three bridesmaids with their respective groomsmen, and then Tiffany. Gone was the punked-out kid with spikey orange hair and pierced eyebrow, and in her place was a graceful and composed young woman. Her hair was a conventional shade of dark blonde, tucked behind her ears and swept off her face in soft waves. Very sophisticated. Aside from the swarm of earrings trailing up her left ear she was very understated. She in no way resembled a giant iris as she feared. In fact she made the dress look classic and lovely and I was proud of my work.

"The dresses are great," Michael whispered and I felt puffed up with pride.

Then the wedding march began and clothing rustled as people stood in anticipation. A little girl in a pink dress stood on the pew in front of us and craned her neck to see. Her eyes sparkled and she jiggled up and down, barely able to contain her excitement. The doors at the back of the church opened dramatically and Danielle and Pete stood, silhouetted against the sunshine outside. The wedding march began and they began the walk down the aisle.

The sight of Danielle in Sophie's wedding dress brought tears to my eyes. In my mind I could see Sophie clearly, all those years ago, looking so lovely on her wedding day where I'd been her maid of honor dressed in baby-blue. The dress looked perfect on Danielle, and I hoped wearing it was an auspicious beginning and that her marriage would be as strong and solid as her parents'.

My mother, Mark and Jill were already at the table when Michael and I arrived at the reception. Pete's sister Stacy and her husband Fletcher were there as well and there was one empty chair, which made my heart ache. It was where my father should have been sitting and I worked hard at swallowing the lump it brought. It was times like those that would grab hold of me without notice and explode the emptiness inside me. Sophie had told me she put Patrick in that seat and I wished he was there now, I wished someone was, just so it wouldn't be vacant.

But he wasn't there. Where was he? Jill was dying to see him. Michael, of course, was not.

My mother looked pretty in a rose-colored suit, her silver hair perfectly coiffed, and she seemed in good spirits. Jill was elegant in a little black dress with lots of chunky silver jewelry. A three-piece combo played chamber music as guests mingled and found their seats and after a while the violinist took the microphone to announce the wedding party. They streamed in; the groom's parents, Pete and Sophie, the bridesmaids and ushers. Tiffany was last with the groom's brother, her new beau. They made a cute couple. He was a few years older than Tiffany, maybe seventeen or eighteen, tall and lanky, handsome in his tux, smiling from ear to ear. He guided them into a little twirl as they entered the room and Tiffany giggled, putting her hand to her mouth. I could see love in her eyes and smiled at them, clapping with the rest of the guests.

Then the big announcement: "And now," (drum roll), "for the very first time, I have the honor of introducing...*Mr. and Mrs. Christopher Sanderson.*" The bride and groom walked in, ecstatic smiles on their faces. Danielle blushed furiously with all the attention but gazed adoringly at her new husband. I felt melancholy watching them. I would never be in their shoes again, getting married for the first time, that new love, the promise it held.

Michael put his arm around me. "That'll be us before long," he murmured in my ear.

We were into our salads of roasted beets, arugula and blue cheese when I looked up and saw Patrick and Pete heading toward our table. I put down my fork and swallowed, hard. Pete had a wide, delighted grin. "Here he is," he said when they got to us. "Finally. Can you believe it?"

Patrick's hair was a little longer than when I last saw him. He wore a charcoal gray pin-striped suit with a bright white shirt and hand-painted tie in vivid hues of red and purple, and looked so handsome it made my throat dry. His smile was wide as he looked at me with lively eyes, and I felt myself flushing.

"Sorry, all," he said. "My plane was late."

He came right over and kissed my cheek. Wariness emanated off of Michael. "Great to see you," Patrick said, squeezing my shoulder. When he took his hand away I still felt its warmth. He extended his hand to Michael and said, "You must be the famous fiancé."

Michael sat up a little straighter, shook his hand firmly and said, "Guilty as charged."

"You're a lucky man," Patrick said.

"Yes, I am." He smiled. "Finally we meet," he said. "I've heard a lot about you." I was surprised by his equanimity. No one would ever guess the snit he had been in about this man.

Patrick moved around the table, charming everyone, including my mother.

"You haven't changed a bit," he told her.

"Well that's the nicest lie I've heard in a long time," she said. "I can't say the same for you," she told him, "but that's because I don't remember you. It's a wonder, though."

He smiled. Then touched her arm. "I'm so sorry about your husband," he said. Her eyes shone with gratitude.

He kissed Jill and Stacy. Stacy grinned hugely. She'd had a crush on him when we were young. "Look at you," she said. "Still handsome."

"Look at you," he said. "Pete's little sis. Still gorgeous." Stacy laughed loudly. She was at least forty pounds heavier than she'd been in high school. "A bit bigger than last time you saw me."

"Who isn't?" Patrick said. "You look great." He shook Fletcher's hand, "Nice to meet you," he said and then sat in the empty chair and everyone picked up their forks. Jill gave me a look across the table. Clearly he'd lived up to whatever expectations she'd had.

Twenty-Eight

"Next week is our anniversary," Stacy announced as we ate our Dover sole. "We've been married twenty-four years."

"Congrats," Patrick said.

"Lovely," my mother said.

"Jill and Mark have been married, what? Twenty-six years? Twenty-seven?" I said.

"Twenty-eight," Jill said.

"How did that happen?" I said. "How'd we get so old?"

"Just lucky," Patrick said.

"Lots of marriage longevity here," Stacy said. "Good karma for a wedding."

"Good thing you're not counting me," I said. "I'm longevity-challenged."

"Well that's about to change," Michael said.

Stacy raised her glass. "Yes," she said, "congratulations." We all clicked glasses. Patrick caught my eye for a moment but I couldn't read his expression.

I wondered what he was thinking. I wondered what he thought about me and Michael as a couple.

The band announced the bride and groom's first dance and they walked out on the dance floor, nearly floating with happiness as the guests applauded. I felt inspired and moved by their shimmer. The band began playing *Can You Feel the Love Tonight* and Christopher took Danielle in his arms. His face was set in concentration and you could almost hear him counting his steps for the first few moments, but Danielle followed him effortlessly. Then Pete cut in, took his daughter in his arms, and Chris went to dance with his mother. We all watched for a while until the band invited everyone to join in. Stacy grabbed Fletcher's hand. "Come on," she said, waving us all forward. I knew Michael didn't want to, I always had to plead to get him to dance with me, but he immediately got up and guided me to the dance floor, leaving Patrick and my mother behind. I watched them over Michael's shoulder, deep in conversation, heads bent toward each other, and wondered what they were talking about. I imagined Patrick telling my mother that he was still in love with me and intended to steal me away from Michael. What would my mother say if that was indeed what Patrick was whispering to her?

"Nice wedding," Michael said.

"Mmmm hmmm," I said.

"Good food. We should find out what caterer they used," Michael said.

"Why?" I said, watching Patrick lead my mother to the dance floor. She put her hand on his shoulder and smiled at him, shaking her head. Patrick took her hand and they moved, slowly.

"Duh…" Michael said, like a teenager. "For our wedding."

The song ended and the band went into *Celebration*. The older people who hadn't had the requisite amount of liquor left the floor and the rest of the younger people poured on. Michael shook his head and shrugged, cutting his eyes toward our table. His dancing skills, such as they were, were limited to slow dances. Rhythm was not one of Michael's strong suits.

"Look at you!" Stacy said delightedly to Fletcher as Michael and I walked away. Fletcher took Stacy's hand and spun her around. She threw her head back and laughed. It was nice, I thought, when you could be surprised and enchanted by someone you'd been married to forever.

My mother and Patrick were still dancing, too slowly for the music, and as we got to them she threw up her hands in surrender, said, "No more," and latched onto Michael's arm.

"Stay and dance," Patrick said to me. Michael looked at him.

"Do you mind?" Patrick asked him, without a trace of irony.

Michael hesitated only briefly before he said, "Of course not," and ushered my mom to the table. I stood for a moment and then I thought, what the hell.

The music's beat thumped loudly as Patrick and I danced through several songs, waves of nostalgia washing over me. The former Patrick and Libby danced in my head, young and strong and so much in love. Patrick's eyes flashed as if he were seeing the same image.

When the band started playing *Hot, Hot, Hot*, he said, "Come on," put my hands on his waist and started a conga line. Soon a long procession filled in behind us and we snaked around the room while Michael sat drinking beer. When we passed him I put out my hand for him to join in but he shook his head so we conga'd right on by.

Sweat dripped down the back of my dress and frizzed my hair. When the band went into *Philadelphia Freedom*, a song we'd danced to in high school, Patrick and I grinned at each other.

"Whew," he shouted over the music, "I haven't danced like this in years. Maybe since this song was new." His hair was damp on his neck and his crisp shirt was wilting but his neon smile made me feel that something was blooming inside me.

"Okay, *uncle*," he said when the song ended. He put up his hands as if he were under arrest. "I need a break, babe." *Babe.*

He guided me to the table with a hand on my back. "Thanks for the loan of your fiancée," he said to Michael when we got to the table. "She about wore me out."

Michael glanced at him, then took a swig of his beer. "You two ought to try out for *Dancing with the Stars*," he said.

"Oh, I love that show," my mother said. "But those dresses the girls wear are so revealing."

I laughed at my mother's oblivion and ignored Michael who obviously had more than a few beers under his belt.

Pete came to the table waving a box of cigars. "Come on guys," he said. "Time for a cigar and brandy in the bar."

"Cool," Patrick said and got up but Michael didn't move.

"Come on, Michael," Pete said.

"Nah," Michael said.

"Come on, man. It's male-bonding time. Let's go get Fletch and Mark off the dance floor. Those guys are gonna have heart attacks if we don't rescue them."

"Yeah, let's go save them with cigars and liquor," Michael said wryly, and reluctantly got up.

When they'd gone my mother said, "I don't think Michael needs brandy."

"He doesn't need a cigar either but I suspect he'll do both."

"He's not very happy about Patrick being here."

"I know. What do you think of him?"

"Patrick? He's charming, of course. I have no memory of him from your high school days."

"You probably blocked it," I said. "Dad would have, too. Back then Patrick was kind of a tough kid with long hair and you know how Daddy felt about long hair on boys."

"Well, he certainly turned out well, didn't he?" She smiled.

"Yes," I said. "He certainly did. You think Daddy'd like him today?"

"Oh I think so."

I pulled the hair off my neck and wiped the back of my neck with my napkin.

"Daddy was crazy about Michael," I said.

"Daddy liked him a lot," she said but something in her tone raised my eyebrows. "He was glad you finally found someone stable. He worried about you being alone."

I remembered how happy he'd been when we announced our engagement. I could picture the pleasure on his face and it made my eyes well up. I wished he were here sitting with us, talking.

"I'm not sure it was Michael as much as *someone*," my mom said, as I took a sip of my wine. I put my glass down. She watched the dance floor intently, fingering her napkin. She knew I was staring at her.

"What are you two talking about?" Sophie said, flopping down in an empty chair, Jill and Stacy right behind her. I was reeling from what my mother had said.

"Mom just dropped a huge bomb on me," I said.

"Oh, honey, I didn't."

"You certainly did."

"What?" Jill said.

"All this time I thought Daddy thought Michael was Mr. Right and Mom just told me he didn't."

"Oh, Libby, that's not what I said." My mother crumpled her napkin and dropped it on the table. "He liked Michael, I told you that. Did he think he was Mr. Right? I don't know. But he thought he was right-enough."

"Right-enough? What the hell is *right-enough*?" I had the urge to get up and walk away. I didn't want to hear any more.

"Libby, calm down," Jill said. "That's not such a terrible thing."

Easy for Miss Perfect to say. "It sounds pretty terrible to me," I said. "It sounds like I'm such a loser that I should just marry whoever will have me." A *loser*? Even to my own ears I could hardly believe the words were coming from my mouth. But it felt as if my beloved father had been disappointed in me and now I'd never have the chance to make it up to him. Unbelievably, tears started rolling down my cheeks.

"No more wine for you," my mother said. When I didn't laugh she said, "Your father thought people weren't meant to be alone, that's all, honey. It had nothing to do with being a loser. You know how he felt about you. He thought you were perfect. He just wanted you to be settled and have someone by your side."

"Lib..." Sophie said, reaching in her bag for a tissue and handing it to me. "No one thinks that. Least of all your dad. He was your biggest fan, you know that."

I wiped my eyes, trying not to smear my mascara. I felt very stupid, sitting there at a wedding, crying like a baby. Where was my decorum? My dignity? I hoped no one else was watching, especially Danielle and her new husband. I hoped Patrick wouldn't walk back in at that moment.

"Daddy always liked you best," Jill said.

We all looked at her. There was a moment of silence. And then I started laughing. We all laughed for a long time, couldn't stop for several minutes, and I felt better after that but still turned upside down. What a strange evening this turned out to be; my mother telling me my father didn't care who I married as long as I married. My fiancé and my high school sweetheart somewhere smoking and drinking together and saying who-knew-what to each other.

So what the hell was I to do about all this? Was Michael my Mr. Right or was I marrying him just to be getting married? Was it better to be married to Mr. Right-Enough than to be alone? And where did Patrick figure into all this mess? I didn't have answers but I knew one thing; I knew that feelings could survive thirty years. Wherever Patrick fit in there was no denying there was still a bond. Was it stronger than the bond between me and Michael? Did it mean anything at all or was it just a fantasy? They say you can't go home again. That's what they say. But I think sometimes you can.

Michael and Patrick came back to the table with cigar smoke wafting around them but seemingly unscathed. Patrick was in high spirits, Michael not so much, but no worse than he'd been earlier. I don't know what I expected. A fist fight? A black eye?

"So have you all bonded?" my mother asked.

"You smell like you have," I said.

Patrick laughed. "Just like Crazy Glue," he said.

His cell phone rang then. "Oh, sorry, I thought I turned it off." He checked the display and said, "Excuse me, I need to take this," and wandered away speaking in low tones. Who was it? Who was so important that he had to answer it in the middle of a wedding reception?

"Come on, Lib. Time to go," Michael said. "Let's go say our goodbyes."

"Oh, let's stay a bit longer," I said. "There are people I haven't even talked to yet." And I haven't found out who Patrick's talking to.

"Your mother's tired," he said. I looked at her.

"I'm fine if you want to stay a bit longer," she said but I could see it around her eyes. Yet I didn't want to leave. I wanted to dance with Patrick some more and laugh and reminisce about old times. Then I saw him on the dance floor with Sophie and couldn't take my eyes off them, heads together, talking earnestly. When they both threw back their heads to laugh at something I wanted to run out there and get in on the fun. And find out who'd called him.

"How about just half an hour?" I said.

"That's fine," my mother said.

"I want to go now," Michael said.

It occurred to me to let Michael leave and take my mother with him and I could get a ride home later with Pete and Sophie. Or with Patrick. But Michael's face was set, his arms were crossed and he stood looking at me, looking ready for a fight. If not for my mother I might have pushed it. But I didn't want to make a scene. And I'd acted like a spoiled child enough for one night so I agreed to leave. But I wasn't happy about it.

We said our goodbyes to the bride and groom, to Tiffany who said, "No, you can't leave yet!" and Pete who said, "Leaving so soon? The party's just getting started."

"Michael's had enough," I said.

Michael bristled. "Katherine's tired," he said.

"It's way past my bedtime," my mother said, ever the peacemaker.

"Oh, I have a feeling you could out-party us all," Pete told her. "Hey, are you coming for brunch tomorrow?" I hadn't planned on it, it was for the out-of-towners, but now that Patrick was here I perked up. "Absolutely," I said.

"I'm not sure," Michael said. "I might have a showing tomorrow."

I was sure he had no showing but didn't care if he did or not.

We stopped on the dance floor to say goodnight to Sophie who was still dancing with Patrick. He shook Michael's hand. "It was great meeting you," he said.

"Yeah," Michael said.

Patrick kissed my mother and told her it was good to see her looking so well after all these years. She hugged him warmly. Then he gave me a peck on the cheek and said, "It was wonderful to see you, Lib." I glowed inside. I wanted to hug him, but I didn't.

"You'll come to brunch tomorrow, right?" Sophie asked. "You too, Katherine."

"We will," I said at the same time Michael said, "We'll see." I felt Michael look at me. I said to Sophie, "Well, I'll be there."

"Good," Patrick said.

I smiled at him and gave Sophie a hug. "It was a fabulous wedding," I said, feeling happier now. "Really fabulous."

Twenty-Nine

When I walked my mother to the door she took both my hands and said, "I shouldn't have said what I did about Daddy just wanting you to be married," she said. "It sounded bad. He liked Michael very much. He thought he was a good man, that he made you happy. We both did." Damage done, I thought, but I didn't want her to feel bad so I kept quiet. "Promise me you won't do anything rash."

"Like what?" I said.

"Like anything," she said. "I can see what kind of mood you're in. Just think things through before you make any decisions."

"Should I pick you up for brunch tomorrow?"

"I wouldn't miss it for the world," she said. I laughed, and was still smiling when I got back in the car. "What's so funny?" Michael asked.

"Nothing," I said.

He backed out of the driveway and headed for home.

"Do you really have a showing in the morning?"

"No," he said. "I just don't want to see that guy any more."

"Did something happen when you all were smoking your cigars?"

"No. I just think he's an asshole."

"*Michael!*"

"Well, he shows up out of the blue and stirs things up. I just think it was inappropriate." he said.

"Oh, Michael, you sound like an old fart."

We drove the rest of the way in silence. I tried to remember back to when the sight of Michael made me glow. I tried to remember when he made me laugh, when we expressed the same thought at the same time. It wasn't all that long ago and I knew it had happened but now I couldn't name a specific time or incident, the memories were like puffs of smoke.

When we were undressing to go to bed Michael said, "I'm not going to the brunch tomorrow."

"Big surprise," I said.

"And I don't want you to go either."

I turned to look at him, his chest bare and vulnerable in the low bedroom light. My fingers paused at the button on my blouse. "Well, I'm going," I said.

His eyes darkened. "I wish you wouldn't, Libby."

"I'm sorry if it bothers you," I said, "but I'm going."

Michael pulled on his pajama top, buttoned it slowly, watching me. "Do you care how I feel?" he asked.

"I care, Michael, but it's irrational." A flush crept up his neck. "It's your problem, not mine. It's a few hours with Pete and Sophie…"

"…and Patrick."

"And Patrick."

"Your former boyfriend."

"It's a few hours and then he's going back to Florida. And everything here will be just the same as it was before."

"Will it, Libby?"

"Why wouldn't it be?" I said.

"I don't know. You tell me."

Tell me you love me, I thought. Tell me how much I mean to you. Tell me I'm beautiful, that you love our life together, that I make your world a better place and you don't want anything to jeopardize that.

"Oh, Michael, stop this. Please. I'm tired. I don't want to play this game. Don't go tomorrow if you don't want to, for whatever the reason. But don't make it my issue. Go show a house. Or not. Go play racquetball instead. Sit here and brood. Do whatever you want to do. But I'm going to pick up my mom in the morning and go over to Sophie and Pete's."

He clenched his jaw but said nothing. He looked at his shoes, at the bed and then back up at my face. He took a deep breath and then he turned and walked away.

Thirty

Bea Rosatti called the next morning at 9:30. "I have a crisis," she said.

"What?" I said, alarmed. Had Dominick had a heart attack? Had she?

"Dominick's kids are having an engagement luncheon for us today and I just put on the dress I was going to wear and it's too long," she said.

Oh, *that* kind of crisis.

"Would you be a dear and come over?" she said.

In my head I quickly calculated how long it would take to drive downtown, find a parking space, get to her condo, measure, hem her dress and make it back to Sophie and Pete's for brunch. If everything worked perfectly I could still be there by noon. What time was Patrick leaving? How much time would that give me before he was gone again?

"Please, honey. I'll pay you extra. I'll give you a big bonus. I'll make you breakfast. With a Bloody Mary. Many Bloody Marys."

I laughed. "Stop. Many Bloody Marys wouldn't help hem your dress."

"So you'll come?"

She was my best, most loyal client. She paid me a fortune.

"I can't, Bea," I said. "I'm really sorry but I have plans this morning."

"Something more important than my dress?" she asked.

"Hard to believe, I know."

"All right, dear," she said. "I guess I can wear the purple one."

I inserted large gold hoops in my earlobes and brushed my hair which was a little flyaway. Tendrils kept springing up around my face but I didn't mind. I patted it down a bit but liked the casual look. I put on a long-sleeved white blouse with satin collar and cuffs, a camel-colored skirt, black alligator belt and black high heeled boots. Way too dressy, I thought, looking at my reflection, but so what? I could always say I was going to a luncheon for the queen afterwards.

Michael was reading the Sunday paper when I went to the kitchen. He eyed my outfit for a long moment, then took a sip of his coffee.

"See you later," I said, taking my car keys off the hook by the door. I bent down and kissed his cheek. If he replied I didn't hear him.

The house was buzzing when my mother and I got there, people all over the place. All the out-of-town guests were there, about 20 of them, and immediate family. Sophie waved from the kitchen and carried a casserole dish to the dining room table which was filled with food and flowers and coffee urns and champagne bottles. Pete walked around pouring champagne. Music played, people talked and laughed. It was a festival of activity.

Patrick was bringing pitchers of orange juice to the table when he saw me and his face lit up, making me happy I'd come. He was wearing the turtleneck we'd bought together when he came to Chicago for lunch. It was soft heather-gray cashmere and looked gorgeous on him. He wore charcoal gray pants, and his black loafers shone within an inch of their lives. He shined them for me, I thought, and grinned at him. He grinned back. "No Michael?" he asked.

"He had a showing."

Patrick hid his disappointment well.

"That boy works too hard," my mother said, although on the way over I'd told her the reason for his brunch boycott.

"Hmmmph..." was all she'd said.

"So nice to see you this morning," Patrick said and kissed my cheek and then my mother's. "You both look beautiful."

"So do you," I said. "Nice sweater."

"Thanks. I can't take all the credit. I had help picking it out."

"Come on, everybody," Sophie called. "Plates are on the buffet. Fill them and find a seat, wherever. Holler if you need anything."

Patrick ushered my mother to a seat on the sofa and said he'd make her a plate if she saved us seats. She said she would if he made her a mimosa.

"She's great," Patrick said as we walked away. "I'm sorry I didn't get to meet your dad."

Patrick's closeness sent little electric currents up my spine as we walked to the dining room.

"Where'd you stay last night?" I asked.

"Here," he said. "On the fold-out couch in the den. We were up 'til three-thirty this morning." He laughed. "I haven't done that since high school." I thought of New Year's Eve thirty years ago. "It was fun. Danielle and Chris were here until three and then had to boogie to grab their bags for a flight at six this morning to Honolulu. They're really fun. It's been a kick getting to know Pete and Sophie's girls."

Sophie had made caramel-apple French toast for the brunch, and several casseroles were filled with her famous egg strata. There was crisp bacon, sausage, fruit salad and mimosas. Iris centerpieces from the wedding were scattered around the dining room.

"Jesus," I said, "when did she have time to do all this?"

"Last night. She was like Rachel Ray on steroids, ordering us around like we were her sous chefs."

I was jealous that I hadn't been part of the fun.

As we ate, my mother grilled Patrick about his life in Florida; what he did, where he lived, how many kids he had, did he exercise, did he cook, did he read the newspaper. I tried giving her a look to get her to let up but she ignored me. Patrick answered easily, not seeming to mind, or even notice, really. He threw questions back at her when there was a millimeter of silence.

When he and I reached for the syrup at the same time, touching fingers, nearly spilling it, I felt my mother's eyes on me, on us. She paused for a moment and then she said to him, "Did you ever think about getting married again?"

I slugged down the rest of my mimosa.

Tiffany wandered through the house with her digital camera snapping pictures, posing everyone in little groups. She tried to take a picture of my mother, Patrick and me but my mother said, "Oh, just take the two of them. I don't like pictures of myself at my age," and she got up and moved off. Patrick put his arm over my shoulder and we leaned our heads close. "Oh, that's cute," Tiffany said, looking at the display. It was.

Tiffany's hair was spiked today and her piercings were in their full glory, filled with shiny hoops and studs. Later she cornered me in the kitchen to tell me that Ryan had asked her to go steady.

"Oh, cool," I said. "Did he give you a ring or anything?" I remembered wearing Patrick's class ring on a chain around my neck.

"A ring? No. But he changed his Facebook page to, *In a relationship*," she said, grinning. I guess that was the current-day equivalent. "He asked me to go to his prom."

"Fun. You can wear your bridesmaid's dress," I said.

She made a face. "Or not," she said. "I'm done with that thing." Then her face softened and she touched my arm. "No offense."

"None taken."

"I *love* Patrick," Tiffany said. "We all had so much fun last night."

"I heard. He likes you, too."

"He likes you, too," she said.

"Why do you say that?"

"He talked about you all night. Asked all kinds of questions about you."

"He did not," I said, but I was pleased at the thought.

"Did too," Sophie said, coming up behind me with a stack of dishes and giving me a bump with her hip. She raised her eyebrows, Groucho Marx style. Tiffany snapped our picture as we laughed.

"Help me with the desserts, would you, Lib?" Sophie said, bringing out large, flat pastry boxes. I unwrapped the goodies and put them on plates, mini-chocolate éclairs, tiny chocolate squares with satiny frosting, cookies, and Tiffany snapped another picture as I stuffed an éclair into my mouth. When she went off in search of other photographic subjects, or maybe her "steady," Sophie said, "He *was* asking a lot of questions."

"About what?"

"Oh, just about what you'd been up to all these years. What you liked to do. If you were going to marry Michael."

"What'd you say to that one?"

"I told him to ask you." She got small plates from the cupboard and the *Danielle and Christopher* napkins. "Are you?" she asked.

"That's the $64,000 question," I said. "Hey, did something happen last night when the guys were smoking their cigars?"

"Pete said there was a little tension but it wasn't a big deal. But Michael apparently made it clear he wasn't about to bond with Patrick."

"I suppose that's to be expected," I said.

"Kind of childish," she said.

"He's jealous. How would you feel if you were in his place?"

"Depends on if I had anything to worry about."
She piled silverware on a big black-lacquered tray.
"Does he?"

"I guess he thinks he does."

Sophie leaned on the granite countertop and
looked me in the eye. "But does he?"

Sometimes when I look at Sophie's face my heart
swells with the familiarity of every angle, every line,
how dear it is to me, how it holds all of our history. "I
don't know, Soph," I said. "I really don't know."

Thirty-One

People started leaving after dessert. Patrick's flight was at 4:30. As he and I picked up dishes, glassware and crumbs from the living room he asked if I could take him to the airport. I wondered if Michael was still at my house, if he was waiting for me. When I hesitated Patrick said, "Pete's planning on taking me so it's no problem if you can't. So if you're busy…"

"No, no," I interrupted, "I can do it. It's no problem. I'd love to, actually."

His eyes brightened. "That's great, Lib. It'll give us a few minutes to chat. We haven't really had any time on this trip."

My mother hitched a ride home with Sophie's parents and when all the guests had gone Sophie, Pete, Tiffany, Patrick and I cleaned up. Pete put on some 70s music and it was like a scene from The Big Chill, all of us dancing around the kitchen, tossing towels to each other, wrapping food, washing dishes, singing to the music.

When *Cats in the Cradle* came on the four of us sang,

Cats in the cradle
And the silver spoon
Little boy blue
And the man in the moon

Tiffany hooted. "What the heck is this?" she asked.

"Harry Chapin!" the four of us said in unison.

"Remember when we went to Purdue to see him in concert?" Patrick said.

"Yeah," I said. "I told my parents I was staying at Sophie's that night."

"And I told my parents I was staying at your house," Sophie said.

"And we stayed in Purdue at that guest house where that lady had four dogs and a big, honking mole on her eyelid."

Our laughter bounced off the oak cabinets, wrapping us all in memories.

"The four of you stayed at a guest house?" Tiffany asked, sitting on the counter watching us as if we were a double-feature.

"Patrick and me in one room, the girls in another," Pete lied. "And don't you try that staying-at-your-girlfriend's story on us. Don't think we won't be checking. We know all the tricks, sweetpea."

Tiffany was smart enough not to answer.

"You sound just like your father," Sophie told him.

"Didn't Randy Cavanaugh and Jess Silver meet us there?" Patrick said. "Remember them?"

"Yeah. I still play poker with Randy," Pete said.

"No kidding," Patrick said. "What's he up to these days? Wait. Let me guess. He's an auto mechanic."

"Nope."

"A roofer?"

"Nope."

"A drug dealer?"

Pete laughed. "No, he's an English teacher."

Patrick laughed uproariously. "Cavanaugh, an English teacher? That's a good one." He ran his fingers through his hair. "He was such a burn-out. What about Jess? Do you know what happened to her?"

"They got married after college and had three kids," Sophie said. "Got divorced about eight years later, married other people, had a few more kids. Then they both got divorced and about ten years ago they married each other again and had another kid ."

"So between the two of them," Pete said, "they have eight kids. The oldest is close to thirty and the youngest is nine."

"Whew! More power to them with all those kids. But that's cool that they got back together again after all those years. Very cool," Patrick said. "But I sure wouldn't want to raise kids today."

"Why not?" Tiffany asked.

"Too old," Patrick said. "Grandkids are just the thing at my age. You get to be the fun one, you get to choose how much time to spend with them, send them off when you're tired and let their parents discipline them. It's perfect." He tossed a pot to me to hang on the rack near my head. And when *Stayin' Alive* came on the stereo he beat out the rhythm with a wooden spoon on Tiffany's knee. Then he grabbed my hand and we did a little disco move. Pete and Sophie joined in and Tiffany couldn't stop laughing.

"You guys are too much," she said.

"She means 'too old'," Patrick said winking, and twirled me. Then we went into the across-the-shoulder-move we did so long ago. Tiffany thrust two fingers in her mouth, let out a shrill whistle and said, "The German judge gives you a 9.9."

I was breathless and wound-up, caught up in the nostalgia of it and the four of us being together again, caught up in Tiffany's admiration. In some ways it felt like old times but in other ways it felt bright and shiny and new. Patrick's hand on my arm gave off sparks that seemed to flutter around and settle on my skin. His face wasn't as familiar as it used to be but his touch was, and his laugh, and the easy way he held me.

When the song came to an end he pulled me close and wrapped his arms around me. "We've still got it," he said. We all clapped and laughed and high-fived each other and Tiffany shouted, "The German judge just changed his score to a perfect ten!"

Thirty-Two

The tollway was clear on our way to O'Hare. Where was traffic when you needed it? At this rate the ride to the airport was going to take sixteen minutes.

"This has been a gas," Patrick said. "Sophie and Pete are just like they always were. I mean none of us look the same but we're the same people inside, aren't we?"

"I'm glad you came," I said. "Sophie and Pete are, too."

"So, you gonna come visit me in Florida?"

I looked over at him and smiled. "That'd be nice, wouldn't it?"

"Then do it, Lib."

"I wish it were that easy."

"I know it's not easy. I know things are complicated for you," he said, and put his hand on my shoulder. "But sometimes we make things more complicated than they need to be. Sometimes the solutions are right in front of us."

"What do you mean?"

"Marry me, Lib," he said, and I almost side-swiped a red Toyota. "Don't marry Michael. Marry me."

"Marry you?" I said. "What's with everybody these days? What's with all this marriage crap?"

He laughed. "Ok, don't marry me. Just come live with me."

"Oh, Patrick. What are you saying? We don't even know each other any more."

He took his hand away leaving my shoulder cold and empty. "We haven't changed," he said. "We know each other like we knew each other thirty years ago. We have the same connection now that we had then." He turned his body toward me, a serious look on his face. "It's like Randy Cavanaugh and Jess. They had a connection that couldn't be broken even though they left each other for a while. Sometimes that happens, Lib."

I couldn't deny what he was saying. I couldn't say it hadn't occurred to me. But there was the other side to that coin as well; the side that said what we had was a high school love affair, that's all, not the real world.

"There's no denying there's still a connection," I said. "But all the living we've done has changed us. We've had these experiences and relationships and all that can't help but change us from what we were back then into who we are now. Yes, maybe basically we're the same people but so much life has to have affected us in ways we can't even calculate."

We approached the departure terminal. Soon he would be on a plane and I might never see him again. I pulled over to the curb. People were bustling around us, getting luggage out of trunks, hugging goodbye.

"Look, Lib," Patrick said, his brown eyes intense. "I love you." He *loves* me? How could he say that? He put his hand up when I started to interrupt. "That's not up for debate. Whether you believe it or not, I do love you. It's clear to me. We've wasted enough time. We're not getting any younger. We've missed out on thirty-some years but we don't have to let the next thirty get away." I felt like my head was going to explode. "So just come and visit me," he said. "Take some time, get away for a little while. Forget the marriage part, I didn't mean that."

"You didn't mean it?" I said trying to sound indignant.

"Well, not for now anyway. Not so long ago I was giving you a lecture about making too many life changes, wasn't I? So we'll take our time. You need some time to heal from the loss of your dad and we don't need to rush into anything. You need to be sure that whatever you do you do for the right reasons. But let's spend some time together, a few days, a week, and see what happens."

"I'm just not sure this is a good time," I said. Why wasn't I saying, *Great! I'm on my way?*

"It's the best time," Patrick said and took my hand. "You owe it to yourself." When he saw the look on my face he said, "No, really, you do. And you owe it to Michael, and believe me I'm not his cheerleader. But if there's even the smallest part of you that's considering it you need to find out, even if it means discovering I'm wrong. At least you won't end up married to Michael and wondering what might have happened."

It was true, I did worry about that. And there was more than a small part of me that wanted to go with him now, right this minute.

He kissed me sweetly, swept the hair off my forehead. "Think about it, okay?"

His face was so close to mine, his breath soft on my face. I felt dizzy. "I will," I said.

He smiled broadly. "That's good enough for me. I'll call you in a couple days, okay?"

"Okay."

"And I'll expect your answer to be yes."

"You will, will you?"

"It's just for a few days. We're not talking about a lifetime commitment. Not now anyway."

I could think of nothing else as I lay in bed that night. I imagined Patrick picking me up at the airport in…what? I didn't even know what kind of car he drove. An SUV? Volkswagen? Mercedes? Rusted-out Impala? So we'd drive in this mystery car through the streets of his town lined with palm trees and pink stucco houses, and pull up in front of his house, which would be what? A house, a condo, a beach shack? I didn't even know. Maybe it was a mansion. Maybe a double wide trailer. I knew nothing about this man.

Would we stand there awkwardly, not knowing what to do or say? And where would I sleep? What if there was only one bedroom? Questions flew through my brain, keeping me awake. I tried counting sheep which, after fifty-five fluffy little critters jumping over an imagined white picket fence, seemed really stupid.

I knew I was going to go even while I knew it would be a huge problem for Michael, an obstacle he might not be able to get past. But Patrick was right – if I didn't I'd always wonder. Chances were so slim that this could work but I had to find out.

It was past midnight when I picked up the phone to call him, past one a.m. his time, but that didn't stop me.

"I'm coming to visit," I said when he sleepily answered the phone. There was silence and I started feeling bad for waking him but then he said, "Mom?"

I laughed and laughed.

"It's nice to hear your laugh," he said in a wide-awake and delighted voice. "I'm so glad you're coming." And then, "Whoa, I better look for my vacuum cleaner."

The pleasure in his voice jumped right through the wires and landed happily in my heart. And then Michael's face landed unhappily in my brain. I would have to tell him, and the prospect of that scene squashed my happiness flat as a pancake.

Thirty-Three

Bright and early the next day I got online and looked for tickets to Florida. I found a good fare and convenient times, and selected a return for four days later. When I got to the screen with the button that said, *Book this reservation*, I had a moment's doubt. Michael was going to freak. One thing was sure, he wasn't going to say, "Oh yeah, I understand, go ahead, spend all the time you want with Patrick. Sleep with him if you need to. I'll be here waiting when you get back."

I hesitated for a second and then clicked the button. *Your reservation is confirmed*, the next screen told me. I raised my eyebrows and smiled. I sent off an email to Patrick with the details of my flight.

I'm nervous, I wrote, **but looking forward to spending time with you.**

Now I had to tell Michael. I picked up the phone. And put it back down. I picked it up again. And then I hung it up again and went for a run instead.

When I got back the red light on my answering machine was blinking.

"Great, Libby." Patrick's mellow tones filled my living room. "Can't wait to see you. And there's nothing to be nervous about. I'll be at the airport, in the terminal outside the gate area, with a big sign that says *CARSON PARTY*. We'll go right down to the beach and have lunch at an outdoor café and drink something with an umbrella in it and eat soft-shell crabs. How does that sound?" I could hear a big smile in his voice. "Bring warm weather clothes. The temps are still in the 80s. See you in a few days."

I did what I always do in times of crisis: called Sophie.

"Well good," she said when I told her what I was doing.

"Really?"

"Yes, really. It's time you did what you wanted to do instead of what everyone else wants."

"Who is this?" I said. "Aren't you the one who told me Michael would be a great husband? That he'd be someone to spend the rest of my life with?"

"Oh, fuck that," Sophie said. "I've seen you and Patrick together. Go. Go see what happens. Michael's not going anywhere."

"He'll be furious. He won't put up with this."

"Yes, he'll say that. He'll tell you you're through, but that's the thing about Michael. He's steady and he's forgiving and he loves you. He'll get over it if you find out Patrick's not the one."

"It seems so cruel to do this to him."

"Well, it's not the nicest thing in the world. But would it be better to marry him and then find out you were in love with someone else?"

"How do I tell him?"

"You say, 'So, Michael, I'm going to go see Patrick in Florida for a couple days and you're not invited.' And then you hang up."

While I was still riding high from Sophie's encouragement I called Michael but got his voice mail.

I said, "Michael, it's me. I know you're pissed that I went to the brunch yesterday. But I expect you'll be over it by Wednesday and be here as usual. I'll make dinner and we'll talk. Okay? Call me."

I didn't hear from him that day.

I had work I needed to complete and deliver before I left; finish the details on a blazer I was making for one client, hem three pairs of pants for another, alter a suit for a third, and work on Bea Rosatti's wedding ensemble. So I put some CDs on the stereo and Andrea Bocelli serenaded me as I stitched in the lining on the black wool blazer. If I moved fast I could deliver it tomorrow and I'd still have a couple days to finish the rest. As I worked I tried not to feel too bad about Michael or too good about Patrick. I didn't know what I'd do if Michael didn't come over Wednesday or call me before Friday, when I was leaving. Part of me thought, *good, I'll just go and not tell him and decide what to do when I get back.* The coward's way out always seems easiest, doesn't it?

Thirty-Four

Tuesday came and went and still no word from Michael. Seemed like a pattern I was on with him, alternating between pissed off and guilty. One minute I'd pick up the phone to call him and the next minute I'd slam the phone down and say, "Fuck you. Two can play at this game."

On Wednesday, though, I went to the grocery store and picked up a whole chicken, some potatoes and fixings for salad. My game plan was to assume he was coming over, thinking he'd have called if that weren't the case. If I was wrong, I was wrong. I sort of hoped I was.

In the afternoon the house smelled comforting with the chicken roasting in the oven, stuffed with onions, lemons, thyme, oregano and parsley. I was peeling potatoes when I heard Michael's key in the door. My stomach did a flip, thinking how I was going to tell him I was taking this trip.

"Smells good," he said, coming into the kitchen, coat still on. He didn't kiss me as he usually did. He barely looked at me. Instead he walked to the cupboard and got a glass, put some ice cubes in it and poured some scotch.

"I wasn't sure you were coming," I said. I cut the potatoes into wedges and put them on a baking pan. "It would have been nice if you'd called me back."

"Yeah, I know. But I wasn't sure what I was doing until I got here." He took a slug of his scotch while I drizzled the potatoes with olive oil and sprinkled them with salt, pepper and rosemary. "I've been thinking a lot about what's going on with you," he said, leaning against the refrigerator, "and I think it must be related to your dad's death." The word brought tears to my eyes but I blinked them away and put the potatoes in the oven. "Grief affects people in different ways. It's a big blow and I understand that. I think it's hard to be yourself right now and I'm sorry you're going through it."

"It is a tough time," I admitted.

"I think you need time to work through that before you can deal with anything else." He seemed relieved to have figured it all out. "I'll be honest, it's not easy to deal with, but I'll try to be patient." I guess I should have appreciated his effort at understanding but I hated how sure he was of himself, how pleased that he'd decoded me. I hated the smug expression on his face.

"I'm going to Florida on Friday," I said. What a bitch.

Michael blinked. He looked into his glass and then back at me, studying every detail of my face as if he wasn't sure who he was looking at.

"It's not just a coincidence that that's where Patrick lives, is it?"

I shook my head.

"Well that's an interesting way to deal with your grief," he said. I had to look away from his eyes.

"I knew it. I knew something was going on. I just didn't want to believe it. Goddamn it, Libby," he said. "I never thought you'd do this to me."

My chest tightened. "I didn't do anything to you. There's nothing going on."

"Yeah, right," he said. "That's why you're going to Florida."

It sounded bad. I knew it did. "Nothing's going on," I said again. "I don't even know how I feel about him."

"You don't know how you feel about him. You don't know how you feel about me," he said, his eyes on fire. "Just exactly what *do* you know?"

"I guess I don't know much of anything anymore."

Michael walked over to the window and stared out. He turned the wand on the mini-blinds, opening, closing, straightening them. "You think he's so great, Libby? You don't even know him." He turned. "You have no idea who he is. But you're going to throw this all away." He threw up his hands, sweeping the room. "Does what we have mean nothing to you?"

"Oh Michael, that's not it."

He watched me for a moment and then he made a huffing sound and turned away. He poured more scotch, adding water this time, and then he left the kitchen.

I stood with my hands on the counter, my heart beating like a jackhammer. The smell of the chicken was intense and I was happy to have something to turn my attention to. I took it out of the oven to see if it was done. When I pierced it the juices that ran out weren't clear so I put it back in. I breathed deeply for several moments and then I went into the living room where Michael was sitting on the ottoman, his head in his hands. Was he crying? He sat utterly still and there was no sound. I wished I could make him disappear so I wouldn't have to see the dejected curve of his back, his vulnerable neck, white where the barber had trimmed his hair. I wished I could spare him this, and spare myself this overwhelming feeling of being a traitor.

I moved Rufus who was curled into a gray ball on the chair, and sat in front of Michael.

He looked up. His eyes were dry, thankfully. "I can't believe this." He laughed but there was no amusement in it. "Two weeks ago I was the happiest guy on earth. What the hell happened?"

I just sat, feeling overwhelmingly sad, for him, for me, for the circumstances, for the fact that my dad was dead. What would my father say if he could see all this?

Michael's shoulders slumped. His face was etched with sadness. "Don't go, Libby."

"Michael..." I didn't know what to say.

"You know how long I was single before I met you? Fifteen years. And I was fine. I figured I'd had my chance and it didn't work out. You know how hard it is to meet someone at our age?" I nodded. "And then I met you." I swallowed. "And you changed my life." Don't tell me any more, I thought. But he went on. "I mean it's not like I didn't have a great life, I did. I had friends, I have a good business, I traveled. And all that was terrific. But you know what? It was that much more terrific with you in my life."

I knew how he felt. I felt some of that myself. It is nicer to have someone to share things with. But the bottom line was I couldn't tell him I wouldn't go see

Patrick. No matter how I felt about him I needed to be sure. I was too old to have regrets.

"You're a hugely important part of my life," I said. "But would you want to get married if I'm not sure? What chance would we have?"

He said nothing. He put his elbows on his knees, head down. I reached out but my hand just hovered over his shoulder, and I withdrew it.

He stood up then, and rolled his head on his neck trying to ease the tension there "I think we'd be fine," he said. "I think once you made the decision you'd realize how right it is."

"I wish I could be sure of that."

"I know." He shook his head, picked up his glass and took it into the kitchen leaving me and Rufus sitting there. In a minute he came back and said, "I'm gonna go."

"Don't leave yet," I said. I thought if we talked it through I'd discover something. Maybe together we'd figure something out. I didn't want him to leave with all this emptiness, and my guilt, hanging between us.

"Why not? What else is there to say?" he said. "You made your decision to go see Patrick. What that says is pretty clear to me, Libby. I don't need an instruction manual to see I'm not on your agenda."

My throat felt tight. Why was I doing this to him? "I'm sorry, Michael, I really am."

He didn't look as if he believed me but he said. "I know." And then he said. "But really, so what?" I flinched from the hostility in his eyes. He sighed, smiled thinly and walked to the front door, head high, shoulders square.

"Are you okay?" I asked.

"I'm fine."

I watched him walk out and close the door behind him and I stood there waiting for him to come back in. I stood there while Rufus wound himself around my feet, but Michael didn't come back. I had a throbbing in my heart, and tears fell down my face and I didn't know who or what I was crying for. It could have been any number of things.

Thirty-Five

Thursday morning I went for a long run hoping it would exhaust my brain enough that it would stop functioning for a while. I didn't want to make any more decisions. I didn't want to overthink what I was doing. Should I go? Shouldn't I? Should I call Patrick and tell him I wasn't coming? Should I call Michael and tell him let's just go to City Hall and get married?

When I ran past my favorite house, Michael's house, I felt sick to my stomach. It could be the perfect home. Michael had no problem spending the money to make it whatever I wanted. Hadn't I always wanted to live there? Hadn't I always said that you'd just have to be happy if you lived in a house like that? As I stood there looking at it I knew that wasn't true. It was just a house. It had no power to make anyone happy.

Jill and I went to my mother's house later in the day. She had asked us to help her clean out the closet and sort Dad's things. "See if Sophie can come too," she'd said. "Dad thought of her like another daughter." So the four of us stared at his side of the closet; all those suits lined up like a chorus line, white shirts, then the blue, shiny wingtips underneath.

"Let's do the dresser first," my mother said. So we opened the drawers and pulled out sweaters, t-shirts, socks. I held his sweaters up to my face and breathed in his smell. How could we give these away when he was still alive in them?

"I'm going to take a couple of these," I said. "Maybe Michael will wear them." I wasn't kidding anyone, Michael was much larger than my father, but no one commented. Sophie stacked handkerchiefs and pajamas on the bed and Jill sorted them into boxes while my mother and I went through his workout clothes; velour sweat pants with matching jackets in varying jewel tones; emerald, garnet.

"Remember when he rode his bike up to the Botanical Gardens?" Mom said. It was at least forty miles from here and he'd set out in the morning with a bottle of water and three granola bars. "It started raining in the afternoon and it was dark before he got back. I was so worried, I was about to call the police when he finally walked in the door looking like something the cat dragged in."

"He was in bed for a week after that with a bad cold," Jill said. "He got lost on the way back but god forbid he should ask someone for directions."

"He was a stubborn one," Mom said with a heartbreaking little smile.

My insides felt as empty as those drawers by the time we moved on to his jewelry box.

"I want you all to take some things," Mom said. There were about twenty sets of cufflinks, rings and pocket watches, pen knives and money clips, some of which I remembered buying for him when Jill and I were little. There was a bracelet made with tiny beads of turquoise and silver that I'd made for him for Father's Day when I was in Girl Scouts. He never wore bracelets (except the day I gave it to him) but he'd kept it all these years. I put it in my pile.

There was a small silver picture frame on his dresser with a picture of Dad with Jill and me when we were about three and five. He was kneeling on the grass with an arm around each of us and we were in matching plaid dresses, our hair in pigtails. I put that in my pile too.

Mom had put out the tea set we'd always loved, the white porcelain one with pink cabbage roses on it, and dainty cups with fragile handles. We sat in the living room in front of the fireplace and drank tea spiked with brandy and told stories about Dad. Like the time he chased the neighbor's dog through the yard in his boxers because the mutt had stolen the newspaper. Or when he decided to be a good guy and do the family laundry and washed Mom's favorite watch; the one he'd given her for a wedding present.

"Can you girls come back tomorrow and help me with his office?" Mom asked.

"Sure," Sophie and Jill said. My mother looked at me.

Uh oh. "Um, I can't," I said. Cuz I'll be in Florida cheating on my fiancé.

"Why not," Jill asked. Sophie daintily sipped her tea.

"I'm going away for the weekend."

"Oh, where are you going?"

To hell, probably. "Florida," I said, boldly, as if there was nothing wrong with this picture.

"What's in Florida?" my mother asked.

Jill's eyes grew. "Patrick!" She said as if she'd discovered gold. "You're going to spend the weekend with Patrick?" I nodded. "Is Michael going with you?"

Sophie let out a little choked laugh and we all looked at her. "Sorry," she said.

My mother drank her tea, knobby fingers grasping the dainty cup, pinky in the air. "What does Michael think about that?" she asked.

"I'm sure he's thrilled," Jill said. "Did you leave the tags on that wedding dress?"

I fingered the sweater in my lap, my dad's sweater, the light blue cashmere one.

"Patrick told me he loves me." The silence was thick around me. Everyone stared. Mother put down her cup. "I know," I said. "It seems pretty silly, doesn't it, after all these years?"

"Wow," Sophie said.

"Jesus," Jill said.

"Oh, Libby," my mother said. Her disapproving tone caught me off-guard and made me feel fifteen. How old do you have to be before you feel like a grown-up with your parents?

"How do you feel about him?" Sophie asked.

"I don't know. Attracted. Confused. Overwhelmed. Guilty. Excited."

"Don't get caught up in this, Libby," my mother said. "He's a very appealing man and I can see how you'd be attracted to him but he's not in love with you."

How did she know? Maybe he was. It was *possible*, wasn't it? "It's absurd," she said. "You haven't seen each other since high school."

I bristled. "Jeez, Mom, one minute you're telling me you think Michael's *right enough,*" I said the words with disdain, "and now when I think you might be right and that I should check this out you say it's absurd." Jill tried to head me off with a placating look but I paid no attention. "Who knows? Yeah, it's unlikely but it's not absurd. Strange things happen in life."

"I just don't want you to throw away your life with Michael for a man you hardly know." She leaned forward. "Think about what you're doing."

"Mom," Jill said but I interrupted her.

"You know what, Mom? I don't need you to tell me how stupid I'm being."

"Libby. I'm not saying you're being stupid."

I ignored her half-hearted apology. "I already feel terrible for Michael and I'm sorry I hurt him. I feel terrible that we've gone so far with the wedding plans and that I bought that dress and that he bought that damn house." I couldn't stop my voice from getting louder. "I should have listened to my instinct in the very beginning and given us both time to think about it. But I didn't and things have gotten out of control and I didn't know how to stop it. And then Patrick came into my life and mucked everything up. But the fact is I have feelings for him."

My mother got up. She looked small and troubled. "Excuse me," she said and left the room. So now I could add her to the list of people I'd injured. This woman who just spent the last few hours sorting through her dead husband's belongings; the man she'd lived with and adored for more than fifty years. What was wrong with me? Why couldn't I just nod and tell her yes, I'd think about what I was doing?

Sophie came over and sat beside me. She put her arm around me and spoke quietly. "Relax, Lib. Calm down. Your mom's just trying to help."

"You mean talk some sense into me, don't you?"

"No. She's just worried."

Jill said, "She wants you to be happy. She doesn't care who it's with. She's just afraid that you'll figure out that Michael's who you should be with and by that time he'll be gone."

"I'm afraid of that too," I said. "But what should I do? Marry him and regret it later? You guys are all making me crazy. You're so wishy-washy, yes Michael, no Michael, yes Patrick, no Patrick. *What*? *Make up your minds*!"

I wished they'd tell me what to do once and for all, step by step, how to handle everyone, what to say, when to say it and how to live with the consequences. Shouldn't life be simple by the time you're fifty?

"It's not our minds to make up," Jill said. "It's yours. Just explain to mom how you're feeling. She'll understand."

"No she won't. My whole life she judged me. She never thought I knew what I was doing. She always thought I should do things differently. I should have stayed married, I should have stayed in my job..."

"No, I didn't," my mother said. I turned to see her standing in the kitchen doorway. "I always thought you were very brave in your decisions because your decisions always scared me." She sat down across from me. "Your father and I just wanted you to be safe. I guess we wanted you to be more like us, more conventional. It frightened us to see you taking so many chances, from the time you were a little girl. You rode your tricycle blocks and blocks before we could catch you, you went out for the hockey team when you could have been a cheerleader, you went to college a thousand miles away, you quit a good paying job to start your own business. It all scared the hell out of us," she said. "We wanted you to be safe and secure. We wanted you to be content. But you never were. You were always moving on to the next thing."

"Is that so terrible?" I said. Tears pooled in my eyes.

"No, sweetheart." She took my hands. "We were always so proud of you. You've lived your life the way you wanted to and you've been successful. You've made some risky decisions but they've mostly paid off and we couldn't be prouder." Now tears were dropping onto my dad's sweater, plop, plop, plop. "Do what you feel is right, Libby. Go to Patrick, if that's what you feel."

"I feel like if I don't check it out I'll regret it for the rest of my life," I said.

"Then go. If that's how you feel then you need to go. You need to be happy. And whatever makes you happy is my happiness, too." She took a napkin off the table and wiped my fifty year old face. "I'm not saying I won't worry, though."

I hugged her, hard. The bones in her back felt sturdy and I let that energy seep into my core. The coziness of the living room consoled me, this room I'd spent my life in, each chair and pillow and doily utterly cozy and familiar. I grew up independent and powerful in this house, confident and strong. I grew up making my own decisions and dealing with the consequences no matter how they turned out.

As if she were tuned in to my thoughts my mother said, "However it turns out everything will work out for the best. You've always been good at figuring things out and working through obstacles that come your way. You're unflappable, Libby. Go. See what happens."

Thirty-Six

Friday. Finally. I hadn't slept much so was up early folding a pair of jeans, some Capri pants and two shirts, and placing them in my suitcase. The weather was in the 80s, Patrick had said. I had no idea what we would be doing. Kayaking? Hiking? Lying on the beach? I threw in a bathing suit and a long skirt that could be casual or dressy with the right top and accessories. The air in the bedroom shimmered around me and I felt lighter than I had in weeks, maybe months. I packed a pair of tan sandals, some black strappy shoes, my running shoes. What else did I need? Something to sleep in. But what? I folded an oversized T-shirt and laid it carefully in my suitcase, and at the last minute I added a sexy, short nightgown. Just in case.

Traffic on the Kennedy Expressway was light and as the taxi sped along I imagined my reunion with Patrick. In my mind I could see him standing there, waiting for me, a big smile lighting up his handsome face. I could see us hugging while people moved all around us smiling approvingly. I couldn't picture what would happen next or where this would lead but I was puffed up with the anticipation of it.

The terminal was crowded as I walked to my gate; business people off to work, vacationers in T-shirts and sandals, families happily heading toward their adventures. I walked briskly, smiling at little children passing by, admiring the glazed doughnuts in the cases along the concourse. Bright sunlight shone in through the windows freshening the tile walls. At the gate the ticket agent told me, "Sorry but I only have center seats left. In the back."

I smiled brightly. "That's great, perfect, thank you so much," I said, as if I'd just scored a front row seat for a Paul McCartney concert.

We arrived a little early into Tampa and I drummed my fingers on the armrest as we sat on the runway waiting for our gate to open up. When we finally parked at the gate passengers stood patiently in the aisles while my stomach fluttered. People who hadn't said a word to each other for two and a half hours now chatted amiably.

"Are you here for business or pleasure?"

"How long have you lived here?"

"Oh, you should try this great new restaurant while you're here..."

"Really? What high school did you go to...?"

Finally we disembarked and I walked through the terminal, moving quickly past slow-moving families and dawdling travelers. Didn't they know I was in a hurry? As I got closer to the main terminal I saw people waiting ahead, just beyond security. There were a number of people of different shapes and sizes, different colors and heights, but I was too far away to see them clearly. The fluttery feeling in my stomach came back and I took a breath to calm myself.

I focused on the woman in front of me, her big butt jiggling softly underneath her silky floral-print skirt. Bad outfit. She should have worn something less clingy with a long jacket. I looked down at my own outfit, gray pants, white blouse, striped vest. Had I worn the right thing? Should I have worn something more feminine? More festive?

I squinted, looking ahead for someone with a handwritten sign but I didn't see him. Maybe he forgot. Or changed his mind. Maybe he had an accident on the way to the airport.

When I got past the security area I stood, searching the crowd, some smiling faces, some anxious ones, occasional shouts of recognition, waving, hugging. But no Patrick.

I waited for a while, tapping my foot, wondering what I'd do if he didn't show up. Perhaps he was waiting outside by the baggage claim area but I worried that if I went down there he'd show up here and we'd miss each other. So I stayed put, trying to be patient. Not my strong suit.

I pulled out my compact and checked my reflection. My face was flushed and shiny, fine wrinkles around my eyes and mouth. I applied fresh lipstick, checked my hair, made sure there was nothing hanging out of my nose or stuck in my teeth, and put the compact away, and then I heard someone shouting, "Libby!" and turned around to see Patrick weaving his way through the crowd, waving his sign. *Carson Party* it said and I laughed out loud.

"I'm sorry I'm late," he said, standing in front of me looking casually handsome in jeans and a salmon-colored T-shirt.

"It takes a real man to wear pink," I said.

He flexed his muscles. "You bet," he said, grinning.

"For a minute there I thought you weren't coming."

"I know, I know. Traffic was nuts. I was going crazy." He wrapped me in a big bear hug, just as I'd imagined. "I'm so glad you're here," he whispered in my ear.

It felt good being in his buoyant presence. He smelled of shampoo and a slightly spicy after-shave. His hair curled softly on his neck. So far so good, I thought. But who knows? Maybe by tomorrow we'd be on each other's nerves. Maybe I'd find out he chewed with his mouth open and belched at the dinner table. Maybe he was a total slob. Maybe he left the toilet seat up.

I laughed at my thoughts and Patrick pulled back and looked at me.

"What?" he said. His eyes sparkled, fine lines fanned out happily in the corners.

"Nothing," I said. "I'm just glad to see you."

He kissed me fully on the lips, a long, lingering, tender kiss that made me feel seventeen. I felt the color rise to my cheeks. It reminded me of the excitement I felt when he kissed me so many years ago. It had made me tingle then with the rightness of it. There was promise in the air back then, a promise unfulfilled. Maybe that was a little of what I was feeling now, even though I knew there was a huge chance it wouldn't work this time around either. But you never knew, did you?

His hand brushed my cheek as if it were made of the most delicate glass. "Come on," he said taking the handle of my rolling bag in one hand and draping his other arm across my shoulder. "I promised you soft shell crabs and drinks with umbrellas in them."

"On the beach?"

"Absolutely."

There would be waves lapping at the shore and the setting sun painting the sky with shades of orange and red. We would toast to whatever this would be. Right this minute it felt so easy and right, like being on a picnic or playing catch in the backyard. But that could change in an instant. If I hadn't come to see him, though, I'd never know. And the thing is you can never go back and do life over. There's no rewind button. If you don't take advantage of the opportunities when they present themselves they're lost to you forever.

I thought of how Michael looked on Wednesday as he left my house, the sadness in his eyes, the straightness of his spine as he walked out, and it made me sad. I knew I couldn't marry Michael because I felt sorry for him, I was pretty sure I couldn't marry Michael at all. But how do you ever know if you're doing the right thing? There are no guarantees no matter how long and hard you think, no matter how many people you talk to, no matter how much research you do. All you can do is make your best guess, forge ahead and hope for solid ground beneath you.

As we walked to Patrick's car I allowed myself a little fantasy of him and me sitting on a porch somewhere twenty years from now in white rockers, sipping steaming cups of tea, companionably reading the paper and looking up to smile at each other. And then the warmth of the sun and the light pressure of his arm on my shoulder brought me back to the present.

What I knew in that moment was that I would enjoy Patrick for as long as it would last; a day, a weekend, a lifetime. And if it didn't work out I knew I would be fine. I didn't need another person to make me happy. Maybe love was in my future or maybe I'd exhausted all the relationships the universe had allotted me. Still, I had a good life, wonderful family and friends, a good job with interesting clients. I had Rufus. Maybe I'd get a dog. I felt a lifting in my heart, and sighed. Patrick smiled down at me making me blush. "It's going to be a great weekend," he said, opening the door of his SUV.

He stashed my bag in the back and then climbed into the driver's seat. He put the key in the ignition and slapped the top of the steering wheel with both hands, a look of pure joy on his face. "Ready?' he asked.

I laughed. "Ready," I said.